PRAISE FOR MARGIE BENEDICT'S NOVELS

NOT MY JOB ANYMORE

Viola is a passionate, witty protagonist who will entertain and inspire readers... Viola's story captivates—digging into the mother/daughter bond as well as grief and loss—and highlights that it's never too late to build courage, face your fears, and start anew.
—*BookLife Reviews by Publishers Weekly*

INVADER

"Fans of sci-fi mysteries and strong female characters should snap up this psychological page-turner."
—*Publishers Weekly*

LAST GIRL STANDING

Fast-paced, entertaining, and exciting, with a fresh, believable voice." —*Kirkus Reviews*

BEFORE THE KILLING

"Mystery fans will love this plot device, which takes a straightforward whodunit to an otherworldly level."
—*The BookLife Prize*

THE THIEVES OF MAGIC

Benedict's "prose is crisp and purposeful, charged with feeling, and always attuned to what will engage readers in each moment." —*The BookLife Prize*

"For those who enjoyed Harry Potter but who seek a feisty, determined female protagonist..." —*Midwest Book Review*

NOT MY JOB ANYMORE

BY MARGIE BENEDICT

FIRST EDITION, MAY 2026

Published by Riveting Reads Inc
Cover Design by Laslo Vanger at 99designs.com
and GetCovers.com

ISBN: 978-1-954584-52-5 (ebook)
ISBN: 978-1-954584-53-2 (paperback)
ISBN: 978-1-954584-54-9 (hardcover)
ISBN: 978-1-954584-56-3 (large print softcover)
ISBN: 978-1-954584-55-6 (large print hardcover)

Printed in the United States of America

For Brian

PROLOGUE

In the last photo I took of Mom, she's giving me the stink eye following my threat to take away her car keys. Somehow this is the picture that pops up on my phone moments before I arrive at the family home, one day after her sudden, inexplicable death.

As my rideshare from Logan rolls to a stop at the curb behind Mom's Cadillac, I rub my twitchy legs. Perched on stilts that suspend it twelve feet above the ground, the house looks as wobbly as I am. But they're the secret to its survival. Instead of slamming against the house, storm waves and the rocks they often carry pass harmlessly underneath, mostly.

The instant I stagger out of the gray sedan, the full-on redolence of low tide revives me like smelling salts in olden times. *Home.* I linger over the view of my beloved ocean smeared with white caps. The sky has taken on a peach hue with the approaching sunset. As for the house, though the siding is filthy and the outer steps creak ominously, I can't resist kissing the stair railing at the top.

I spend a minute digging my set of her keys out of my purse only to have the door yield to my touch. When I was growing up, we always left it unlocked, but times changed and after a break-in across the street, Mom vowed to start using the bolt. What she said and what she did rarely matched, however.

Steadying myself at the entry, I swallow the *I'm home!* at the tip of my tongue. The shadow of approaching evening darkens the rooms, except for one lit hallway in the back. For a moment I can't move, overwhelmed by the hollow sensation working its way outward from my heart to my home to my entire world. "Mom!" I call out. The silence of her non-answer is more jarring than any sound.

I need to move. With suitcase and purse abandoned by the door, I explore the kitchen, shiny from the three-year-old remodel. When I lived here as a child, we had pine cabinets, formica counters, a linoleum floor. The windows were small, unlike the current floor to ceiling ones and the sliding glass door leading to the deck. Mom used to prepare frozen dinners while Keaton and I did paint by numbers in our coloring books at the wooden table. She hated cooking but the house had to be spotless. Today is no exception. Surfaces are wiped, floor mopped, dishes cleaned and put away.

In her bedroom, the bed is made, blinds raised, dirty clothes in the hamper, and robe hanging in the closet. A library book, a historical account of a disastrous sea voyage, rests on her bedside table. I check the drawer for her cell—*nope*—and use my phone to start a list of items to track down.

Mom's burial outfit hovers behind her other clothes in the closet. An attached note, worded with her usual dramatic flair, says "The last thing I'll ever wear." There's a red Merino wool blazer, with the pin Dad gave her for their fiftieth anniversary stuck into the right lapel. It depicts her favorite car—a Cadillac —outlined in small diamonds. The black pants are also wool and the blouse is white silk. Aside from these, the bundle includes a white bra and panties, nylon knee-highs, and black Jimmy Choo high heels that she couldn't possibly have worn.

The fancy dress with the geometric pattern that I admired during my last visit—*missing*. I add it to my list.

Mom's aura is strongest in the family room, which is why I saved it till last. At the threshold, my insides quiver with the expectation of finding her alive. The sight of her empty yellow recliner—the throne from which she held court—slays me. My eyes fill and tears spill out. On the table beside the chair rest unopened bills and a half-full glass of water. Yesterday's newspaper is on the couch open to the crossword. Before completing it, she would have read every page. It's like she left the room minutes ago and her chair is still warm to the touch.

Between bouts of weeping, I watch her seat as if a determined stare might still cause her to appear. Of course, with or without Mom, the dusty yellow—used to be lemon yellow—recliner stands out like a banana poking out of a sand dune. It has nothing in common with the rest of the beach-themed room, splattered with driftwood carvings, conch shells, and Andrew Wyeth prints. A high ceiling and broad windows invite visitors to recline on plump turquoise pillows, contemplating the hypnotic ocean, nearly invisible now with the sun already set in late afternoon.

Eventually I approach the chair and run my hand over its inner surface. It resembles a paper mache cast of her body after thirty or so years of daily use. The way it hugged every part of her precisely must have been the secret to its supreme comfort. That and the velour fabric that's softest where it's most worn down.

I lean closer, trying to catch a whiff of the violet scent Mom usually wore. Her love for the flower even led her to name me *Viola* because it sounded similar. But instead of something delightfully floral, a smell I might generously describe as *vintage musty* hits me straight up the nostrils.

I grab a tissue from the box on the side table and honk my nose into it. When I toss it into the wastebasket, the drawer, left partway open, draws my gaze. Inside rests an envelope with my name on it.

My mood changes abruptly when I take it out and read the full text of what Mom wrote: "To be opened by Viola Sagewood Bluff upon my death." Good god, she labelled what might be her last communication to me like it was a major turning point in an Agatha Christie novel. Naturally, the envelope was sealed in hot wax. I wonder why she didn't stamp it with a skull and crossbones.

I know my mother well enough to guess this missive contains way more drama than I want to address right after losing her. Why my whole name written out? Who else but me, her only surviving child, would enter her house and discover this letter in the drawer beside her chair, while her body awaits cremation at the funeral home?

Of course, curiosity will drive me to open it. This and my inability to ignore a command from my mother, even when she can no longer voice her disapproval. But sensing my life will be different after reading it, I linger over the text, admiring her cursive handwriting. The image of Mom at her desk flashes before me. Her hand swirls, creating the beautiful circular flourishes of the capital letters by the dim light of a flickering candle on a cold winter's night.

A sudden shiver rattles me. This too is a cold winter's night and the heat is not set high enough. I rise to adjust the thermostat, turn on more lights, and make myself tea. Ten minutes later I'm back in the family room with steam floating above my cup and a Milano cookie on my saucer. Sitting on the couch, I dip my cookie and stare out the window at the lights of an airplane passing through the blackened sky.

After the last lazy sip of my drink, I retrieve Mom's letter and glance at the writing once more. Flip it over and gently pull open the flap, trying not to tear it. I slide the letter from its sheath and unfold it. The thick paper, Mom's favorite cream stationery, is the product of a bygone era. The satisfying feel of it, along with Mom's full name and address embossed and centered at the top, cause a warmth to spread through me.

The warm sensation dissolves as I read the letter. I read it again. And again until the page slips from my trembling hand. I could never have imagined its contents. If, right now, Mom rose from the dead and rode past the window doing a handstand on a flying carpet, I would be less astonished than I was reading this confession.

1

———————

WHEN MOM GOT ME A CAR

There wasn't any question who would "help" me pick out my twenty-first birthday gift. Dad was a professor of mathematics at Boston University and probably never held a torque wrench in his life, whereas Mom grew up in Grandpa's repair shop and could change a tire by the time she turned twelve.

We set out in her shiny, Hatteras-blue Cadillac Seville on a Saturday morning in October. You would've thought Mom was going to dinner at the Ritz, not shopping at a used car dealership. Every excursion gave her an excuse to dress up. She wore high heels, her lightweight Austrian wool coat, and a hat that was popular at the time, shaped like an upside-down dog food bowl.

She pulled into Pro Ride on Washington Street first, but when the salesman gave her a sideways glance and asked where her husband was, we drove away.

We went to Best Value Used Cars next but burned rubber on our way out after the salesman began explaining how the carburetor worked to Mom, who certainly hadn't asked him. I was wishing I could have gone alone or even with Dad, who couldn't tell a Chevy from a Datsun, when we sidled into the third place, Manny's in Twisted Creek.

I winced at Manny's signature billboard with the slogan, "Prices that will blow your mind." The artwork pictured seven or eight people looking astonished, probably because the top of their heads had exploded, with smoke and flames erupting out of them.

"Classy, Mom," I said.

"Hush."

"Can you ignore the salesman's comments this time?"

"I don't trust any business that condescends to women."

I sighed and followed her inside the showroom, where a young man who looked not much older than me approached. At first I thought he resembled that Jehovah's Witness guy who, when he came to our house the year before with a brochure, Mom slammed the door in his face. Like him, the salesman was clean-shaven, his hair was parted like he took a ruler to it, and he wore a suit and tie.

The slick outfit couldn't hide that the salesman was a hunk as we used to say, with black hair, broad shoulders, and a mischievous smile that made me go all melty inside. *Don't say anything to demean women*, I quietly prayed.

"We're looking for something reliable and reasonably priced for my daughter's first car." Mom gave him a fierce look that challenged him to question her qualifications as anyone's car advisor.

Thank god he didn't. Instead, he introduced himself and offered us coffee. Unlike the previous two salesmen, he made polite conversation by complimenting Mom on the Seville and asking if I was in college. When I told him I had recently graduated, he asked what kind of work I was looking for.

I said something like, "I love art."

"He means a career, Viola," Mom said. "She took computer classes. It will probably be a job related to that." She made it clear she wasn't interested in chitchat by leading us back outside.

The salesman asked what kind of art I liked.

"Murals are my favorite." Remembering I had a photo of one I worked on in college, I pulled it out of my purse to show him.

"That's really powerful. You're very talented." His words caused a sort of glow to spread through me, though I understood he might be buttering me up for the sale.

"What are you working on now?" he asked.

Mom's disapproving glance silenced us and reminded the salesman to get back to business. "What kind of car are you looking for?" he said.

I jumped in before Mom had a chance. "A VW Beetle." I had spotted an adorable red one when we turned into the lot.

Mom was aghast. "A Beetle?"

Its shade had drawn my eye like a pyromaniac to flame. Crimson was the color of sunsets, roses, and revolution. It would perfectly encapsulate my image of myself as nature lover, artist, and nonconformist. Plus the car was small enough not to tax my parallel parking skills.

"The red one is in terrific condition. Hardly any miles on it." The salesman turned toward where it was parked.

I matched his pace with enthusiasm, but now Mom trailed behind. A moment later she paused and said, "I'd like to look at this Dodge Dart."

I followed her gaze to a puke green car that strongly resembled whatever Grandma owned and sometimes drove through town at fifteen miles per hour.

A flicker of apology flashed in the salesman's expression before he shifted his attention to Mom. He must've been sure he'd lose his job if he didn't follow the most likely source of payment.

"The Dart received a perfect five-star rating from the National Highway Traffic Safety Administration," Mom said.

"I like the Volkswagen better," I said.

"The Beetle has an excellent reputation for safety too," the salesman hedged.

Mom ordered me over to the Dart and insisted I look inside. The salesman opened the door and showed us its features. "Would you like to take it for a test drive?"

"Yes," Mom said. We took turns driving around the block, then my mother popped open the hood to examine the engine compartment. While she questioned the salesman about everything from gas mileage to when the tires were last rotated, I wandered over to stare at the red Bug. It had a soft gray cloth interior and a decal of a dove on the dashboard.

Mom came from behind and put an arm around me. The salesman hung back, giving us privacy to discuss the purchase.

"The Dart is in good condition and I talked the price down," Mom said. "I know you like the VW, but they have some issues. Poor safety features, limited crash protection... the engines aren't very powerful, the car handles poorly at higher speeds, there are concerns about its electrical systems... and they have rust problems." She pointed out a small section of rust behind the right rear fender.

"I love the color," was all I had.

"Reminds me of the lollipops you always picked at the doctor's office." Her statement had the intended effect of establishing who was the child here. I bowed to her sound reasoning and agreed to let her purchase the Dart.

When we turned back to the salesman, he was staring at an older man in a plaid suit who gave him a come-back-here wave through the showroom window.

"Can we go to the office now?" the salesman said.

"Let me get a picture first. It will just take a minute." Mom kept albums of photos marking first events, like when my brother and I took our first steps, ate solid food, said our first words, started school, and on and on. Since this was the first car buying event, it would be important to include the salesman.

She stood by the side to get the full length of the car in the photo, while the salesman and I were to stand by the driver's door shaking hands on the deal. "Sorry about my mother," I said under my breath. The moment could not have been more awkward, with me feeling ridiculous and him looking worried, watching the man in plaid come out the door and head toward us with furious steps.

The rest is a blur. There was the vroom of an engine, and the sight of a car speeding toward us. The feeling of myself being yanked to the side and landing briefly in the salesman's arms. The sound of an explosion, the stench of burning oil. The confusion of police and EMTs arriving, directing us out of the way and arresting the driver who miraculously stumbled out of his fractured car. The flash of a photographer's camera— not Mom's this time—taking our pictures.

My mother remained frozen across from me, her mouth open in an expression of horror. No doubt she was imagining what could've happened if I hadn't been whisked out of the way.

We learned later that the intended victim had been our salesman, who was also a manager despite his youth and had recently fired the driver of the car that nearly obliterated us. While we were on the lot, the ex-employee had called the dealership, threatening to kill his former manager. Police had been notified, and the older salesman had tried to wave our guy back into the showroom without jeopardizing the sale, naturally.

The dealership offered to gift us another Dodge Dart, an exact match for the one that was totaled, right down to the puke green color. I tried to convince Mom the car was a bad omen—she fully believed in signs and omens—but she was so delighted over the prospect of a free car, she insisted the Dart actually saved our lives. Her explanation was that posing in front of it had allowed the salesman to be looking in the direction of the approaching murderous car.

We had to sign a document pledging never to sue them for our having almost been killed on their lot, and in return, I got to own a vehicle that gave me flashes of PTSD every time I climbed into it.

I didn't think Mom could ever arrange a worse pairing than this. I underestimated her.

2

——————

WHEN MOM GOT ME A HUSBAND

Anthony and I met two years after the used car lot debacle. At twenty-three I was just out of my third failed relationship following college. It ended by mutual agreement the day after I canceled a dinner date with Jon so I could huddle alone by the TV, slurping Boone's Farm, competing with Jessica Fletcher to be the first to solve the latest killing in Cabot Cove—a murderers' den if ever there was one.

Around the same time, Mom's dear friend Camilla had her first grandchild. My mother took a slew of photos and babbled over them whenever I was around. She also used my old baby clothes as the source of unrealistically adorable stories about me, while pretending to pack the outfits up for donation.

I was her one hope for extending the family line. If only I would get serious about finding a boyfriend who hadn't been fired from two jobs in a single month (Robert), wasn't living in his parents' shed (Art), and whose eau de toilette wasn't *essence of weed* (Jon). Though my brother Keaton had not yet come out to us, the ballet class he enrolled in the second he hit college sealed Mom's opinion that he must be gay. To achieve her goal, she would need to focus all her attention on me, especially now, after I had already failed more than once to identify proper husband material.

It didn't take long after Jon's departure for Mom to propose having lunch with me at Sage Corner in Cambridge. When I suggested a different restaurant, she nixed it by faking a craving for something I couldn't even find on Sage Corner's menu. "They make it if you ask for it," she assured me.

"I think I'll ask for lobster newburg," I said.

She pretended not to hear me.

When we arrived at the cafe, she rushed ahead toward the hostess, who was handing menus to two customers.

"Janis?" Mom said to the woman.

Janis turned to her with exaggerated surprise. "Rosemary? How are you? It's been a while. You here for lunch too?" She wore a gray sweater with black slacks and a navy-blue silk scarf. In time I learned this was her uniform. Her clothes existed on the grayscale, except for the scarf which would always be a serious color like teal or burgundy—never anything frivolous like white or yellow or heaven forbid pink.

"Fancy running into you," Mom said. "We must like the same food. This is my daughter, Viola. Is this your son?"

"Anthony," Janis's son said, not waiting for her introduction. He stepped forward and shook my hand. His smile showed me this phony setup hadn't fooled him either.

I was taken with him. He had height, sandy brown hair, good teeth—not a given for anyone back then—and ears that stuck out enough to be endearing, not clownish. Later I learned he was six years older than me, but he looked young for his age.

"Would you like to join us?" Janis asked like the idea just came to her.

Mom inserted a dramatic pause. "If you're sure we won't be intruding."

"Not at all."

Neither of them pretended to care what Anthony and I

thought. They maneuvered to have us sit side by side at the table.

"Anthony, I heard you teach at Harvard," Mom said. "You must be quite the scholar."

When Anthony didn't speak up to confirm or deny the compliment, Janis said, "He certainly is. When he first got the job, he was the youngest assistant professor they had ever hired in the Ancient History department." I eventually understood that Janis lived vicariously through her son. She was among the millions of women in her generation who graduated college only to discover most professions still weren't open to them.

Anthony being an academic explained everything. Mom had a thing for college professors. After all, she had married one herself. She was convinced anyone at Harvard must be a well-mannered genius unlikely to get sucked into a lifestyle involving alcohol, drugs, or loose women.

"Quite the coincidence our running into you," I said.

"What are the odds?" Anthony said.

"Oh, you know, friends like to eat at the same places," Mom said, throwing me a cut-the-sarcasm look.

Anthony didn't seem to mind. He appeared eager to get to know me. He asked where I lived—on Beacon Hill in a unit shared with my friend Diana—and he told me he lived by himself in an apartment in Cambridge. He wanted to know what I did for a living, and was interested to hear I worked as a technical writer at Digital Equipment Corporation, known as DEC.

"That's unusual for a woman, isn't it?"

Mom's face flashed with annoyance and I wondered if Anthony had sunk his chances with me. "Only because women have long been blocked from entering science and technology fields," she said.

"I agree, it's completely unfair." This instantly restored him to my mother's good graces. Turning to me, he added, "I really admire you for breaking in."

I can't recall the rest of our conversation, only that at the end, with our mothers hanging back to give us privacy, Anthony shook my hand, holding it a moment longer than before, and asked if he could have my phone number. I didn't hesitate to jot it down on a napkin for him.

He called that night and we went out the following evening. Though it would've been faster if we'd taken the subway, he drove to my apartment and presented me with a dozen red roses at the door. I leapt up to receive them and had to restrain an impulse to run down the hall, knocking on doors to show all the neighbors my spectacular bouquet. No one had ever greeted me with flowers on a first date before.

He brought me to a French restaurant on trendy Boylston Street. The personal sommelier who arrived to explain the wine selections and my napkin being refolded during a visit to the ladies were evidence it was miles out of my price range.

"Let me order for you," he said when I picked up the menu.

"Um...." I had my eye on the beef bourguignon.

"Trust me? I'd like to get some plates to share."

"Sure. Sounds fun." As long as he was treating.

Mussels arrived for our first course. "Take it out with your fingers." Anthony showed me.

I put the whole thing in my mouth like he did. Maybe I just had a mental block, but it felt like eating a slug. I struggled not to make a face.

"Now you can use the empty shell as a pincer to eat the others."

Lucky me. I forced myself to swallow another.

"Don't forget to slurp the juice out of the shells."

"Mm." I made a pretense of doing that.

In his excitement, he didn't notice my lack of enthusiasm

until the waiter came to take our bowls. "You didn't finish," Anthony said.

"I need to save room to try everything."

He let it go. It was our first date.

The conversation surged during the remaining courses. He attacked all the big topics like politics and religion and the nature of being. Like him, I gave my opinions openly, and we sparred playfully a few times over our differences. It felt like a test of my intellect and my ability to discuss sensitive subjects without taking offense. When I looked at it that way, it became a challenge. I didn't like settling for less than an A+.

I had never met anyone like Anthony before. He was brilliant, sophisticated, confident. When I looked at him, he shimmered like a sparkling star in a velvet sky.

The meal took three hours. Afterward he drove me home and walked me to my front door without angling for an invitation inside. He asked me for a second date but didn't kiss me. I looked at my feet to hide my disappointment.

The kiss arrived a week later after dinner at his house. We had sex for the first time that same night.

Eventually he met Diana, my roommate. I didn't see it then, but now, when I picture that day, I remember how different his manner was with her than with me.

She came out of her room wearing bright red lipstick, black leather pants, and a tight-fitting jersey with her boobs nearly popping out. After the introductions, she said in her South Boston accent, "Don't forget we're goin' to PJs tomorrow." Turning to Anthony, she added, "Hey, why don't you come too? You play pool?"

He wore a look of horror, as if she'd asked if he loved skinning rabbits. "No, I don't play."

"Well, you drink, don't ya?"

"Not at bars."

"Just alone in your apartment?"

He looked down and pulled at his sleeve.

"Just kiddin'!" Diana slapped him on the back. "Hey, I'll get outta your hair." She grabbed her jacket and left us alone.

He said, "What does she do for a living?"

"She's a secretary for a big firm."

Years later, Anthony would tell me he thought she was a hooker. "Ah," he said. "Where did she go to college?"

"I'm not sure. I think she just did secretarial school."

"That makes sense." He said this in a pleasant tone that carried a subtext of, *I could tell she was an idiot.*

Diana was, in fact, one of the smartest people I knew. But from that day on, I placed myself above her. Our friendship was never the same.

I married Anthony six months later, before I understood that anyone who wishes to be loved by a star must be prepared to fall into their orbit.

Over the next forty years, significant milestones occurred. Our daughter Max was born seven years after we married. Stanford hired Anthony and we moved to the California Bay Area. My brother Keaton died tragically from AIDS in his thirties. Lung cancer took my father when he was eighty-three.

Then Mom died.

3

WHEN I'M SIXTY-THREE

The day my mother died, I was up early for coffee followed by a walk around our neighborhood of artful homes with harmonized shrubs and symmetrical trees. Even in January, something was always blooming, thanks to daytime temperatures that often climbed into the sixties. I knew I ought to be grateful for the mild weather, the tranquil environment, and our cream-colored stucco home with burgundy shutters. Stanford University, where Anthony worked as a professor and head of the history department, provided a generous housing subsidy. Without this, we would be in a tract home in Central Valley with him commuting round trip four hours a day.

But as I finished my loop and turned onto our front walkway, my chest tightened. I wasn't sure when I first began having this sensation, but I knew it only happened when Anthony was home. What else could I do but ignore it? I pushed into the house, directly to the kitchen, where my husband was eating the last few bites of poached eggs over buttered toast with a side of bacon.

"Morning," I said.

"Where've you been?" Translation: *why weren't you here when I needed you?* Anthony knew I was out walking. I always walked in the morning.

"Switzerland," popped into my head.

He made a sour face.

"I had to return the cheese because it had holes in it." It wasn't my best joke, but merited a groan at least.

"You used to make breakfast for me."

"I've grown weary of domestic servitude."

"What if I grew weary of supporting us?"

"I'm happy to accept that role if you take over the household jobs." I knew there was zero chance of his ever agreeing to this.

"You couldn't earn the money I do," he said.

"Not with that attitude."

"It's just the reality, Vi." He glanced at the clock. "Got a meeting." He wiped his mouth with his napkin and dropped it on the counter before leaving the kitchen.

I glanced around at his used dishes on the table, the food-splattered counters, the poaching pot, and a fry pan full of bacon grease on the stove. "I'll just leave these for the maid, shall I?" I called out after him.

His footsteps continued toward his study in the back. Why did I bother with the sarcastic comments? He pretended not to hear them. Or maybe his brain had learned to subconsciously filter them out. How convenient that must be for him. If only I had a vision filter that kept me from seeing his messes. *Why are these dirty dishes still on the table?* he would ask at the end of the day. *What dishes?* I would answer in all honesty.

I ate granola with raspberries while scanning the news on my laptop. These days it was enough to confirm nothing had changed drastically since the day before. When I finished my meal, I loaded the dishwasher, hand washed the pans, and wiped the countertop. "Thank you, Vi," I said, imagining the words coming out of my husband's mouth. This never actually happened, because Anthony believed love means never having to say *thank you.*

Things were better when he always worked in his office on campus. These days he only went in two to three times a week, during quarters when he had a class or two to teach. Today he was working at home, composing a book about Hannibal's invasion of Italy. The way he brought something fresh to a subject that had been covered countless times impressed me. If only he would apply that same single-minded determination to his role as my partner in this marriage.

I took my shower before gathering the pile of clothes Anthony had deposited on the bathroom floor and starting a load of wash. With no other chores for the moment, I headed to my home office that doubled as a guest room to work on my computer.

A text arrived from Anthony: *Today is garbage day.*

I texted back, *Every day is garbage day when I'm with you, darling* 🖤.

No reply.

It was almost time for the truck to arrive, so I rushed outside and dragged the two cans to the street. I saw my neighbor's husband doing the same. He often brought our empties back to the garage for me. I could tell he thought Anthony was a dickwad for never doing it himself.

I returned to my office. I was taking an online class in graphic design and my instructor had sent me feedback on my latest homework, creating the logo for my future graphic design business. Last week, I'd spent hours rejecting names like *Designs by Viola, Viola Creates,* and *Voilà Viola* before settling on *The Art of Viola.*

The artwork had followed quickly. Above the words, I did the barest sketch of a viola resting horizontally, showing its outline on the top and fading out on the bottom. At first glance it resembled a naked woman stretched on her side. I was beaming as I read my teacher's email—she thought it was a sexy, eye-catching design and had only two small suggestions for improving the typography. The clenching in my stomach relaxed a bit as I dove into the next assignment, designing the home page for my business website.

The work went well, I forgot to eat lunch, and the afternoon flew by. At four-thirty my calendar reminded me we had plans for tonight and I headed to Anthony's office to remind him.

"We've got the party at Nico and Claire's at six-thirty."

He looked up from his computer and scowled. "Do we really need to go to that?"

"We'll get free gourmet food and premium wine."

"I thought you didn't like them much."

"Your pronouns are confused."

"Weird time of year, just past Christmas and New Year's."

"I guess they should've waited for Martin Luther King's birthday," I said. "Hello? It's a housewarming party. They liquidated their stock options to build their dream home in Woodside. Aren't you curious?"

"A little." Victory conceded, only because, like me, he wanted to see if money could buy happiness.

As we showered and dressed, I remembered what I wanted to ask him earlier. "Did you get a chance to consider the bid from Lopez?" I had placed the proposal for remodeling the downstairs bathroom on top of Anthony's keyboard.

"The price is ridiculous," he said.

I sucked in a deep breath. "Compared to...?" *the estimates you refused to track down*, I didn't say. "They do amazing work. You saw Sheila's bathroom. I called two other references and they all raved about the quality. How responsive he is. How clean they left the work site at the end of every day."

"We ought to get a couple more estimates."

"Go ahead. Get all the estimates you like."

Anthony hated making phone calls, and had passed the job of estimate-gatherer to me long ago. But I'd already spent considerable time vetting Lopez and don't relish putting in another day researching more companies—reading their reviews, checking their licenses, calling references.

He slipped into silent mode while we finished getting ready, always a sign of his disapproval.

It was well after dark when we turned onto Nico and Claire's street off Skyline Boulevard in the Santa Cruz Mountains. Before we could enter their driveway, a teenager who barely looked old enough to light a campfire waved us to the side of the road. We handed over our keys, trusting he held a valid license to park our car.

Drawn by the bright lights inside and out, we walked the rest of the way to the house—I mean, mansion—gaping at the enormity of it.

"Incredible," Anthony said.

"Yeah. It's like, modern and rustic at the same time."

"And the trees..."

Majestic redwoods surrounded the estate, blocking any possible view of neighbors.

"What'd you say Nico does?" Anthony said.

"He's a senior engineer. Claire too."

"We picked the wrong professions."

We followed a young, heavily tattooed couple into the house. The inside was equally spectacular. The kitchen had granite countertops, custom cherry cabinets, plank flooring, and the latest in intelligent appliances, though personally I preferred to be smarter than my refrigerator. Every window had a view of the scary forest. There were three bedrooms with plush bedding, and an art studio that made me envious because Anthony had always quashed any suggestions I had for adding one in our backyard. As far as I knew, Nico and Claire were not even artists.

We returned to the living room, where Anthony cut the line at the crowded bar to fetch himself a glass of cabernet.

"I'm not pregnant," I said when he rejoined me.

"What?" He gawked like I was out of my mind, though I was obviously joking. Menopause was a distant memory for me.

"There's no reason I can't drink wine," I translated.

"Oh. I wasn't sure what you wanted."

"Let me introduce myself. I'm Viola, your wife."

The milling guests parted for Nico making his way toward us. He looked the same as always, like a giant six-year-old with messy hair, wearing flip-flops and a T-shirt that said *Friction is a drag*. To look at him, you'd be sure he still lived in his parents' basement.

"Hey Viola, how are you?"

"Great. The house is amazing!"

"It's very nice." This was raving by Anthony's standards.

Nico wrapped me in a bear hug before asking, "How's retirement?"

"I miss you guys. But I like my graphic arts class."

"When can we hire you back?"

"Ha, I'm done with tech writing."

"I mean as a graphic artist."

"She's enjoying her retirement," Anthony said.

I masked my annoyance for his presuming to be the expert on my thoughts on retirement. As far as I was concerned, you didn't call it retirement when you were planning on going into business for yourself. "You remember my husband Anthony?"

"Course. History professor, right? I love history. What are you working on?"

This was the magic question that always brought Anthony to life. He began an animated discussion of his latest work on Hannibal. I was about to wander off when someone bumped his arm from the side and he accidentally spilled wine on his shirt front and the carpet. "What the hell?" he said to the poor woman who hadn't seen him.

"Sorry." She scurried away.

"Viola, can you help?" Anthony said.

I ran to the kitchen and grabbed a roll of paper towels, moistening a few sheets at the sink before racing back to the scene of the spill. Anthony continued explaining his book to Nico while I wiped the wine off his shirt and the floor.

When I returned to the kitchen to throw away the dirty towels, I found Claire watching. Unlike her husband Nico, she looked different than when I last saw her. She had let her hair go gray, cut it short, and added a green streak that matched her eyes. If you gave her a cape, she would look like a pixie super-hero for the fifty-plus crowd.

"Do you ever get tired of it?" she asked.

"What do you mean?"

"Being his handmaid?"

My face burned. It was true Anthony made zero attempt to help with the cleanup of his own wine on his own shirt. While his minion—me—did all the work, he barely paused in the lecture he was delivering to Nico. I stung with embarrassment, wondering how many other guests might have witnessed my humiliation. At the same time, I bristled at Claire's condemnation. Who was she to criticize my relationship with my husband?

Her expression softened. "Hey, I'm sorry." Putting her arm around my shoulder, she led me into the empty art studio. "I didn't mean to hurt your feelings. Right now I'm especially sensitive to the shit husbands do."

"Why?"

She lowered her voice. "Has Nico told you?"

"Told me what?"

"We're separated. I'm renting a place in Los Gatos."

"But you just built your dream home."

"It was horrible," she said. "We couldn't agree on anything. Several times I almost bashed him on the head with a heavy tool. Once he nearly knocked me down the stairs. I was pretty sure one of us wouldn't survive the construction."

"But it's done now. You can move on. Don't you want to live in this gorgeous place?"

"This was Nico's dream. I hoped I would learn to love it. Instead I freaking hate it. I grew up in San Francisco. I like being around people. This place is so isolated, it creeps me out. Nobody can hear you scream, you know?"

"Why are you doing this party?"

"We planned it months ago. We couldn't get our money back if we cancelled. So I said, *fine, we'll have the party and you can show off your house.* He's buying me out."

"Wow. I'm really sorry."

"I'm not. I'm happier than I've been in years. Why do we do it, Viola?"

"Do what?"

"Suppress ourselves. I don't know, maybe you don't. But a lot of women do. I should've left him years ago. I always supported what he wanted. What about me? Now I'm living the life I want. We don't have kids. I can be completely selfish."

"You don't think you'll be lonely, living by yourself?"

"I love the freedom. I'm making new friends. Life's too short, you know? Why should we settle for anything less than joyous? I'm fifty-two but that still leaves lots of time for new adventures."

I was dazed listening to her. *Life's too short.* I'd been having similar thoughts lately, but I couldn't picture myself doing anything so drastic.

On the way home, Anthony said, "Nico told me they're getting divorced. Can you believe it? They built that beautiful house and now Claire doesn't want to live in it. Jesus. Talk about ingratitude."

"They both have money. It's not like this was some sort of gift."

"I always thought she was weird. Do you think she's a lesbian?"

I suppressed a laugh. This was Anthony's way of accounting for the behavior of any woman he didn't understand. "Must be," I said. "What other explanation could there be?"

WHEN DID *bitter sarcasm take over my life?*

An hour after returning from the party, I lay awake in bed, my thoughts punctuated by the wild boar-like grunts of Anthony's snoring. I wondered when exactly it happened that my subconscious abandoned the possibility of reasoning with my husband, and latched onto snide one-liners as the only form of communication that might save me from the descent into madness.

He never called me on it. He probably viewed me as a child letting off steam. He was clever enough to say nothing as long as I continued to run our lives smoothly.

My phone flashed with the notification of a call coming in. I checked to see if it might be our daughter Max, but it was an unknown number. However, the area code was the same as my mother's, making me wonder if she might be using a friend's phone to reach me. Worse, someone might be calling on her behalf. With a sense of foreboding, I sprang from the bed and hurried out to the hallway to answer the call.

4

—————

SHE DIDN'T SUFFER

"Hello?" My voice wavered.

"Is this Viola Bluff?" The serious tone of the unfamiliar male voice unnerved me. If it was a robocall, they had definitely changed their approach.

"Yes." I reached my office and balanced on the edge of the chair.

"This is Dr. Henderson from Wexton Hospital. You're not driving, are you? I have something to tell you."

My heart skipped a beat. "Is my mother all right?" *Who is Dr. Henderson?* A horrible vision flashed before my eyes, of Mom unconscious and bleeding at the bottom of her outdoor stairs. I had tried so many times to get her to move from that deathtrap of a house, to no avail.

The man spoke with the assurance of someone who made these sorts of calls routinely. "I'm sorry. Earlier this evening, your mother collapsed getting up from her table at a restaurant. The EMTs arrived quickly and did all they could, but they couldn't save her. She was gone before they reached the hospital." He paused and added, "She didn't suffer."

I lowered my head and squeezed my eyes shut in confusion. What did he say? I struggled to wrap my brain around it.

"Viola?" he said. "Are you still there?"

"Are you sure it's my mother?" My voice sounded small and distant. "Her name is Rosemary Sagewood." I clung to the hope they mixed up someone else's contact information.

"Yes." His voice was patient. "Rosemary Sagewood. I'm terribly sorry."

"What happened to her?" *He told me she collapsed, didn't he?* It was so vague, so unspecific.

"She probably had a stroke. It would take an autopsy to confirm it, but typically we don't do autopsies on the elderly, when death has occurred from natural causes."

"What should I do?" They say your life flashes before you at the instant of death. I didn't know yet if this was true, but images of my mother's life flashed before me right now. I saw her youthful and carefree, then older and sterner, up to the last few years, when she became childlike again, full of mischief and laughter.

"Contact O'Connor's Funeral Home in Windset tomorrow. The hospital plans to move her there in the morning, according to the directions from her primary care doctor. Is this correct?"

"Yes. Thank you," I said, because my mother taught me always to use my manners, no matter how dire the situation.

Directly after we hung up, I woke Anthony.

"Huh? What is it?!" Whenever he was woken unexpectedly, he always snapped up in a panic, like he was expecting to be surrounded by Russian gangsters.

"It's Mom. She's... dead. She died."

"Your mother?" Anthony's mother had passed two years ago. "Dead? How is that possible?"

"Um..." I was too upset to sarcastically explain the inevitability of death. "She had a stroke."

"She was so healthy."

"Not anymore."

He squeezed my hand. "I'm sorry, Vi."

I felt a terrible pressure inside my head, like an overfilled balloon ready to burst.

"Come to bed," he said. "There's nothing you can do right now."

I massaged my temple. "We need to call Max."

"What time is it? She'll be sleeping."

Our daughter lived in Brooklyn and worked as a stagehand for the musical, *The Book of Mormon*, on Broadway. "Doubt it. She'll kill us if she finds out later we didn't call right away."

He knew Max well enough not to argue about this.

I put the phone in speaker mode. Anthony leaned back on his pillow and closed his eyes.

Max picked up after three rings. "Hey Mom, what's going on?"

"Did I wake you?"

"Of course not. But why are you up?"

I actually wanted to know what kept *her* up till nearly two am her time, but I restrained myself and told her what happened to her beloved Grandma.

"What? NO." She burst into loud sobs. "How could she die? She was so full of life!"

Max was close to my mother. She also had lost out on landing the lead in her senior high school play for being too dramatic. "I thought she'd live to be a hundred!" Max was bawling. I heard a male voice near her asking if she was okay. "My grandma died," she told the man.

"Tell me she didn't suffer," Max said.

"No, sweetie. The doctor assured me. We'll be doing a viewing in Windset in a few days. Can you make it?"

"Of course I'll be there!"

Someone else in the background asked what her order was. They aren't kidding when they say New York never sleeps.

"I have to hang up, Mom. I'm here with someone."

"Who?" Even in my grief, I wanted to know who she might be seeing.

"Gotta go! Love you! Give Dad my love!"

He and I said, "Love you too," in chorus as the phone went dead.

I pressed my hands against the sides of my head, trying to stifle the painful throbbing.

"What's wrong?" Anthony said.

What could possibly be wrong after my mother just died and my head feels like it's going to explode? There seemed no point in saying this out loud, though.

With no answer from me, he dropped back on the pillow and a moment later he was snoring. I took two tablets of acetaminophen and lay down in my study for twenty minutes until the pounding in my head dissolved into a dull ache.

Returning to the bedroom, I poked Anthony awake. "I have to book our flights."

"For god's sake, it can wait till tomorrow."

"We need to leave first thing in the morning. Dead bodies don't last forever, even with embalming. She told me she wanted a viewing. I need to notify people. Arrange it with the funeral home. Publish her obit. Handle everything to do with her will and trust. Get the house ready for sale." Mental pictures of the tasks spun inside my brain like whirling dervishes.

"I can't go," Anthony said. "Department meeting tomorrow." He called department meetings *the dullest events on earth* and typically jumped at the chance to avoid them.

"Come in a couple days then," I said. "I could use your help."

"I have to check my schedule. How long will you be gone?"

"I don't know. Might be months."

"Months?" He frowned. "How am I going to manage?"

"I have no idea. But Nico has a smart refrigerator that might be able to help."

5

THE LAST TIME I SAW HER ALIVE

Waiting for my plane to take off, I recalled my last visit home only a month ago in December. I had sprawled on the family room couch staring through the back window at the birdbath on the deck, imagining mice hockey players using it as their ice rink. When I shifted my gaze to the wider view, the crisp edge where emerald sea met pastel sky reminded me of a similar dividing line between my point of view and Mom's.

"I never tire of looking at the ocean." Mom typically watched the horizon with the intensity of a pining lover awaiting the return of her long-lost sailor.

I breathed in the aroma of my coffee. She and I needed to talk about matters related to her health before I would fly back to San Francisco. Since my arrival, I'd seen her reaching for furniture to steady herself while she shuffled through rooms. As unsteady as she'd become, she might easily lose her grip on the railing outside and plunge down the staircase that ended at a concrete landing at street level. Mix in the occasional patch of ice on the steps this time of year and it was a disaster cocktail.

"You're taking your life in your hands every time you go out the door," I said.

"I'm not worried. If I fall, I'll go quickly."

"Why don't I find this reassuring?"

"Plunging to my death is an easier option than the boat. I won't need your help with this one. And they won't be able to charge you with murder. That was the only problem with the drowning plan." Mom insisted she didn't want to stay alive if she got Alzheimer's. Her brilliant plan was for me to take her out on a boat, attach an anchor to her, and shove her overboard.

"You might not die in the fall," I said. "You might just break all your bones and be racked with pain for the rest of your life."

"Then go to plan B, the boat. Problem solved."

In the evening, she sat writing in a notepad for an hour before telling me she had something to "go over" with me.

I poured us each a glass of chardonnay and settled beside her. She made a production of spreading the notepad on her lap. "I know you think I'm a burden so I've written out my death plans."

"Death plans? I never said you were a burden." My first thought was that Mom had devised yet another harebrained scheme for assisted suicide—more like matricide—if she got dementia.

"I'm only trying to be helpful," she said. "I made a list of what you need to do after I die."

During her lifetime, Mom had never so much as trusted me to adjust the thermostat. Why should death be any different? After informing me which funeral home to call—the only one in town—she told me to contact friends and family with the news of her demise.

"You're right, Mom," I said. "I never would've thought of that."

"I've listed them here with their phone numbers."

"Who are the family?" I was the only real family left.

"Your father's two cousins are still alive."

"Right." My mother hadn't spoken to them in years, but sure, I would try to reach them using what must be thirty-year-old landline phone numbers.

"After you write my obituary, submit it to the Globe right away. I might've left out some people on my call list."

"Sure, Mom."

"You'll be proud of me that I already picked out what I'm wearing for the viewing. I set it aside in my closet, pressed and ready. You'll just need to send it over to the funeral home."

"Your viewing? What about the Mass?"

"We're not doing a Mass.

"But you're Catholic." She had clung to her childhood religion despite that Dad, Keaton, and I were all agnostics.

"No I'm not."

I stared at her, wondering if this might be the strongest sign yet that she had dementia. "When did you give up your religion?"

"I don't know. It's been a gradual process. Can we get back to the plans? I'm having a viewing, that's all. It's nice seeing the deceased one last time to say goodbye. And O'Connor's does a good job embalming. Then later in the year you can do a celebration of life. More people will come if you give them time."

"Whatever you say."

"I want to be cremated, then you can dump my ashes at sea like your dad and brother." She tore off the piece of paper and placed it in the drawer beside her. "The list will be right here."

I turned away so she didn't see me rolling my eyes. We might not need to "dump" her for years if she would only follow my advice for taking better care of herself.

When she was in the bathroom, I got curious about the outfit she picked out for her viewing and went to her bedroom to check her closet. Sure enough, a beautiful new satin dress covered in clear plastic was hanging separately from her other clothes. The colors were slate blue and silver in a geometric design. Mom had always been stylish; she used to run a fashionable dress shop.

"What are you doing?" she said from behind me.

"I wanted to see what you picked out. It's lovely."

She narrowed her eyes at me. "That's not it. My death outfit is in the back of the closet with a note on it. I don't want to be staring at it every time I walk in here. It's depressing to be reminded you have two feet in the grave. Can we do this another time? I'm pooped."

"Sure." I wondered why she seemed annoyed. She usually loved showing off her clothes. "I do like that dress. When are you going to wear it?"

"I don't know. My friends are dropping like flies. Every other week there's a funeral."

The dress looked too showy for a funeral, though. I prickled with curiosity. I knew my mother well enough to guess there was something she didn't want to tell me.

The last day of my visit, a sensation of dread overwhelmed me at the thought of leaving her to manage on her own. With Dad and Keaton gone, there was only me to watch over her. This week alone, three times she forgot to turn off the stove after making tea, twice she received second-notice bills in the mail, and once she called me *Mittens*, the name of her cat who died last year.

Despite my best efforts, Mom refused to give up driving. "I've always been a better driver than you," was her constant refrain. "My father taught me when I was eleven." I held my breath and clutched the side armrest as Mom drove over pedestrian walkways past parents and children attempting to cross, and when we came screeching to a stop inches from the descending train barrier.

But when I brought up these issues, Mom insisted she could still handle them all, and that what I observed only happened *this one time*. She would not let me take over the paying of bills, and she would not give up her car, and rather than ever moving to assisted living, she would sooner thrust a blade into her belly like any good Samurai. "I've never minded the sight of blood," she reassured me.

When the Uber arrived to take me to the airport, Mom joined me at the door holding a piece of paper.

"Call me if anything comes up," I said. "I can fly right back if you need me. How about we get someone to come over a few hours a day?"

"Ugh. You know how I like my privacy." She placed one hand on my cheek and gazed into my eyes. "I'm a big girl, sweetheart. Your husband needs you more than I do."

"He thinks he does. I wish you'd let me do more for you."

"I don't want to be any trouble."

The statement was so far from the truth, all I could do was laugh. Mom had not agreed to a single request, any one of which would greatly reduce the amount of trouble she was. But it was a testament to the closeness of our relationship that each of us knew exactly what the other was thinking, and this made Mom laugh out loud too.

Later it comforted me to remember the way we clung to each other, shaking with laughter, more like two sisters than mother and child. As we broke apart, and I snatched up my suitcase, she pressed the folded sheet of paper into my hand and said, "Put this in the obit. They're my final words on the subject."

"The subject of what?"

"Everything."

6

GAME OVER

I put together Mom's obituary on the plane ride back to Boston.

Rosemary Brooks Sagewood passed of natural causes on January 10, 2025. Survived by her daughter Viola Sagewood Bluff (Anthony) and her granddaughter Maxine Bluff, she will be hugely missed by all who knew and loved her.

Born in 1935 in Chicago, Illinois, Rosemary was a feminist trailblazer. The only child of Norman and Beth Sagewood, she insisted on learning car mechanics from her father, who owned several auto shops. But after discovering no one, not even him, would hire her as a mechanic because of her gender, she became a passionate advocate for women's rights. She left home at eighteen, the first in her family to attend college.

At Boston University, Rosemary studied business management and became engaged to Thomas Sagewood, an acclaimed PhD student in Mathematics. They married a week following their graduation, and she remained devoted to him throughout their lives together.

After moving to Thomas' beautiful hometown of Windset, MA, they bought a house overlooking the ocean. Two children arrived before Rosemary started her own business, a dress shop called La Femme, located in Twisted Creek, MA, and renowned for its high-fashion outfits for special occasions. She amazed her friends with her ability to perform greasy car maintenance one day, and transform into a stylish, high-heeled bombshell the next.

All her life, Rosemary adored entertaining and hosted legendary parties. In 2004, when the Red Sox broke their 86-year losing streak, she invited the entire town over to celebrate. She continued the tradition in 2007, 2013, and 2018, and have no doubt, the next time they win the Championship, she'll be pouring champagne in heaven.

Inspired by her love of The Game and the words of Hunter S. Thompson, Rosemary's last cadenza in her own life story was this:

"I skidded sideways into the grave like it was home plate for the final World Series, clothes shredding, bones crunching, screaming, 'Game f—king over, baby!'"

It was good I finished writing the obit before arriving at the house. Because later, after reading her letter, I couldn't think of a single nice thing to say about her.

7

MOM'S DESPICABLE LETTER

To be opened by Viola Sagewood Bluff upon my death.

DEAREST VIOLA,

I don't even know where to begin. There's something I need to tell you and I should've done it years ago, but I didn't because I'm a coward. I almost broke down and told you while you were here, but I just couldn't bear to face your anger and disappointment.

Please keep in mind I could've gone to my grave without saying anything and you would have remained blissfully ignorant of something that happened so very long ago in the past, it shouldn't concern you anyway. Then why am I telling you at all? I've noticed changes in you ever since Covid when Anthony started working at home a lot. The way you talk about him, I don't know what's going on, but you just don't seem happy. Once I thought he was the perfect husband for you, and that's why I've always encouraged you to hang in there following some of your minor spats. But now I'm wondering if I misjudged him.

If I'm really being honest, I have to say the Catholic in me is a tiny bit afraid of damnation. They sure know how to instill the fear of judgment in their flock, so that even years later when you no longer go to confession or even attend church, you still feel it. Will a postmortem confession help? It can't hurt.

I know what you're thinking: "Mom, could you please get to the point?" Well here it is. I met Anthony six months before you did. I went to a history lecture he gave at Harvard. Your father didn't want to come, naturally. Whenever anyone talked about history he fell instantly asleep. Anyway, after the lecture, which had painfully low attendance, I went up to ask Anthony some questions. We got into a great discussion but since we were kicked out of the lecture hall, we had to continue at a bar down the street. When you're in a bar, you order drinks, right? Yes, we had too much to drink. One thing led to another and next thing I know, we're in his apartment doing the deed. I feel so ashamed writing this. I was about twenty years older than him and married. But I bet at this age you can understand the temptations we women sometimes feel to stray. Your father had his own dalliances, but that's another story.

That was it. Nothing more ever happened between us. Neither of us wanted to repeat the experience.

But while we were in the bar, I bragged about you a bit and showed him your picture. I guess he found you interesting but hesitated at the awkwardness of asking this older woman he just had relations with to introduce him to her daughter.

But after a few months passed and I had made it clear I wasn't interested in a repeat performance, he called and asked if I'd mind arranging for him to meet you. At first I told him no, I couldn't believe he was asking. Shades of "The Graduate," you know? But when I considered it further, it occurred to me he was great husband material. The man is brilliant, you know that. And he's been steady like I thought he would be. No drugs, not much alcohol. Always brought in a decent income. Good father to your daughter. Never cheated so far as we know.

Yes, he had a one-night stand with an older woman before ever meeting you, but how many men past the age of twenty haven't had all sorts of hook-ups before landing the woman of their dreams?

A week later, I called Anthony back and agreed to arrange the meeting. You seemed crazy about him. The past seemed irrelevant.

What happened between him and me before he even knew you shouldn't have any bearing on your relationship. At the same time, it seems unfair that we hid this key information from you and you likely would've made a different decision about whether to marry him had you known. Because of this, I feel at least somewhat responsible for your marriage being in an unhappy state now.

Neither Anthony nor I ever meant to hurt you or anyone through our one night of thoughtless actions. I hope you can move past this and rediscover your love for your husband. But it's up to you now since I'm gone.

Please find it in your heart to forgive me. Despite all my flaws, I loved you with every particle of my being and only ever acted in what I believed to be your best interest.

Mountains of love from your dearly departed Mom

8

——————

FUCK IT NIGHT

Wat the fuck.

Mom and Anthony. Anthony and Mom. No wonder they were thick as thieves. It makes me want to throw up thinking about it.

The letter is packed with despicable content, starting from their liaison. She offers no apology for being married when it happened, making me wonder how many other times she might've cheated on Dad. Then there's the offhand remark she tosses in about his infidelity, and here's me thinking both my parents were true to each other throughout their marriage. How could I have been so blind?

She didn't even confess for my sake. The letter is her Hail Mary attempt to escape eternal damnation, but her obvious lack of real remorse probably has her dancing with the devil right now.

And Anthony... he makes me sick. Imagine sleeping with an older woman, then asking to be hooked up with her daughter. What kind of pervert does that? I know the daughter leaves her wedding to run off with Dustin Hoffman at the end of "The Graduate," but I remember the look on her face at the end, like *who is this person and why did I just pick him over the steady guy at the altar?*

I kick Mom's chair. "How could you not tell me?"

I hear her voice replying: *Because I knew you'd explode, just like this.*

"You should've told me before I started dating him!"

Obviously you would never have gone out with him after that.

"Exactly! What is wrong with you?"

Well, to begin with, I'm dead.

"THIS ISN'T FUNNY."

I itch all over, like an army of ants are crawling on me. I scratch my torso, my arms, my legs. I have to get out of here. The sun has set; there must be a bar open somewhere. I grab my winter jacket, then pause and look down at myself. I'm wearing a flannel shirt, cargo pants, and wool socks. Add a beard and suspenders and I'd be Jeremiah Johnson. There's an easy solution, though. Mom's my size—time to raid her closet.

Fifteen minutes later, I emerge victorious in a miracle bra, sexy cleavage-revealing top, black slacks that are tight on my ass, and jewelry with the unifying theme of *maximum sparkle.* I smell like Mom after applying her floral-scented hairspray to tame my long brown hair with gold highlights, and when I check myself out in the full-length mirror, I'm surprised how much I resemble her too, at least the way she looked at my age.

To wrap up the flaunting package that is *me* I choose Mom's classic gray wool coat with the faux fur lining and her supple leather boots that pinch my toes in a way I know I'll regret later. I'm uncertain whether I'm committing an act of rebellion or if, after death, my mother has completed the process that consumed most of her life, of replacing her daughter's persona with her own. In the ultimate irony, I nearly die exactly the way I predicted she would, when on leaving the house, I trip on the steps outside and barely stop myself from flying headlong onto the concrete.

Unfazed, I start the Cadillac and gun it toward The Old Oaken Tavern. My friends and I used to get in with fake IDs when we were seniors in high school. At times it seemed like everyone over the age of sixteen was packed in there, mainlining the hard liquor at the dimly lit bar, while a wicked fire spat in the massive stone fireplace.

On my way there, Mom's letter keeps replaying in my head and a knot forms in my stomach as I wonder if Anthony ever mentally compared me to her in bed. *Gross*, the thought is disgusting. Mom is right, I would never have let him near me if I knew. With the knowledge I have now, despite that it's ancient history, I don't want him ever touching me again.

With a start, I realize it was not our two mothers, but rather him and my mother who set up the "accidental" meeting between us at the sandwich place in Cambridge. Yet he pretended to be amused over my poking fun at our moms arranging it. What a phony. What an asshole.

I veer into the tavern parking lot and do my best to shove Mom's revelation out of my head to focus on the present. The place looks the same as I remember—wood siding painted dark red, with ye olde English lettering on the tavern-y sign that hangs in front. New Englanders prefer establishments that haven't changed their look since 1688.

When I open the car door and my wedding diamond glistens in the streetlight, my stomach heaves again. I wrench off the ring scraping skin in the process, and almost hurl it in the storm drain, but the thought that pawning is still an option stays my hand. Shoving it in my purse, I charge into the building, not stopping till I reach the hostess stand.

I look around. Oh my god, what has happened to this place? Only three people are at the bar, and they're all alone, drinking themselves into oblivion by the looks of it. Two elderly couples occupy tables. One pair picks at their shared chicken entrée; the other awaits the arrival of their food in gloomy silence.

"Table for two?" the hostess asks, though I'm clearly standing by myself. I guess she can't imagine a woman eating at a restaurant alone, whether she's divorced, widowed, or avoiding her husband who slept with her mother.

"One. But I'm still considering." I glance back toward the sound of new people arriving. The woman, shuffling with a cane, opens the door for her husband, bent over a walker. "Why don't you help them first?" I say to the hostess.

Is this what I have to look forward to? It's like the Ghost of Christmas Yet to Come has delivered me here to view the horror that awaits me if I don't change my ways. I stagger back to the door, flee to my car, and lean against the side window gulping for air. *Does a panic attack feel like this?*

There must be someplace livelier in the area; it's a Friday night, for god's sake. My old friend Jackie would know. In high school, she was always dragging me into outrageous hijinks. We last saw each other at the thirtieth reunion, fifteen years ago. Sometime between then and now, we texted each other our cell phone numbers, but for some reason I'm hesitating to call her.

This is *anything goes* night, I remind myself. Time to make a pact with myself to do whatever I want, no matter how unhinged, for the rest of the evening. Beginning with the call to Jackie.

She answers on the third ring. "Viola?"

"Yup, it's me."

"I was hoping you'd get in touch. I heard your mother passed. I'm really sorry for your loss."

"Yeah, whatever." The fury still burns inside me over her betrayal.

"Somebody got mommy issues? I can relate."

"Don't ask."

"I'll leave it for your therapist. How long are you here for?"

"I don't know. However long it takes to sort things out." A sudden thought hits me. "Are you still a divorce attorney?'

She gives a bitter laugh. "Divorce puts the worst of human nature on display. I was constantly depressed. I'm in a creative field now. I run my own business framing pictures."

"That's so cool. I'd love to talk more about that. By any chance are you free tonight? I have a need to go out and party."

"Oh yeah? Come with us then. Ken and I are heading over to The Sound Wave in Kelham."

"I can't crash your date with your husband."

"We're not married. We met on thehopefulromantic dot com."

"A dating app? I keep hearing about those, but I can't imagine doing it."

"They're a game-changer for people our age. Your sex life used to be over if you got widowed or divorced. First time I went on the app was an eye-opener. Lots of regular guys looking for women their own age, can you believe it? Who knew?"

"Are you and Ken serious?"

"Who cares? I've had three divorces already. I'm just looking to have fun. Come with us. A local band is playing tonight."

Fuck it. "Fine, I'll meet you there."

My GPS guides me to the town of Kelham and into the parking lot at Longfoot Beach, across the street from The Sound Wave. When I get out of the car, I hear the ocean lapping the shore and I'm tempted to walk on the sand. But that's the old Viola talking. Tonight I'm busting out at this joint.

"Cash only," the burly guy at the door tells me. I guess they haven't heard of Venmo. Luckily I'm still in the habit of carrying a few twenties at all times.

The cloying scent of weed clings to the place. The dim lighting can't disguise the dated furniture, the chipped paint, the scuffed wooden floors. But the atmosphere is lively, with most of the customers mingling in groups around the bar. The average age is probably fifty plus, though I glimpse a smattering of twenty and thirty-year-olds. There's a small town, everybody-knows-everyone vibe. Walking in feels like slipping on my favorite pair of old slippers.

I spot Jackie at a table with a gray-haired man who looks like a cuddly bear in a green and blue wool sweater that I bet his mother knit for him.

"Hey sister," I call out to her.

"Vi!" She jumps up and locks me in a hug.

"You haven't changed a bit," I say. This is of course an exaggeration, because everyone changes enormously in going from eighteen to sixty-three. But still, she looks good, with pure white hair in a stylish short cut that reminds me of the actress Judi Dench, only Jackie is younger and slenderer. Her smile is dazzling, which could only happen through the miracle of teeth whitening and Invisalign. She has suspiciously few wrinkles, which gets me speculating whether she had a facelift or just Botox injections. What a weird age this is, where we spend half our time wondering what work our friends had done.

Since I haven't done anything, I doubt she's doing much speculating about me, but she says the kind thing and insists I haven't changed either.

Ken proves to be as cuddly as he looks, rising to hug me as soon as Jackie has backed away. "I feel like I know you," he says.

"I've been telling him the stories," Jackie explains.

"I deny everything." Not wishing to butt in on their date, I excuse myself to get a drink. It takes a few minutes to squeeze in through a gap and order a martini, something I reserve for special occasions. Tonight is a special occasion—my declaration of independence.

Sipping my luscious drink, I glance back at Jackie and her beau. They touch each other a lot. She rests her hand on his. When he returns from the restroom, he grasps her shoulders from behind and leans over to kiss her before sitting back down. For heaven's sake, they play footsie under the table. It would be gag-inducing if they had been together for decades, but instead it's cute. I can almost picture them as high school kids instead of oldsters. There's a playfulness and sexual tension between them—two qualities that disappeared from my marriage long ago.

It might be the excitement of getting out on my own, or the remembrance of my high school escapades with Jackie, or the anticipation of the band about to play, but somehow I feel youthful tonight. When I check my reflection in the bar mirror, I'm surprised how young I look, though it's probably just the low lighting in here.

"Hey." An attractive man gripping a whiskey is suddenly beside me. He's middle-aged, with sandy-colored hair, a black leather jacket, jeans, and cowboy boots. "Are you a friend of Jackie's?"

I nearly choke on my drink with surprise over anyone noticing me.

"Saw you talking to her earlier," he says. "She's a great lady."

"I know. We were high school friends. How do you know her?"

"I'm Freddie, her dentist." He offers his hand and we shake.

"Seriously?"

He gives me a half smile. "I get that a lot. What about me screams *not a dentist*?"

"The leather jacket."

"I should've worn my white coat?"

"Definitely. And a headlamp." I try not to open my mouth too wide, lest he spot any of the imperfections that no doubt need work.

"What would you guess I do?" he asks.

I scrutinize him. "Town mayor."

"Dude."

"I mean specifically, Kelham's town mayor. It's always been the cool town. You know, where the bad boys are."

"And the bad girls?"

I shrug.

"What's your name and what do you do?"

"Viola. Take a guess."

"With a name like that, must be something related to music. Lounge singer?"

I laugh. I'm feeling light-headed as I gulp down the last of my first martini to make room for the next. With my permission, Freddie orders me another.

"It would explain your good looks," he adds.

Good looks? I'm sixty-three. My good looks didn't follow me into the last decade. I make a mental note not to call him if I need emergency dental services, because he's obviously blind.

"I was a tech writer for Google before I retired," I say. "For my next act, I hope to become a graphic designer."

"Stop hoping. Just do it." Our drinks arrive and we clink glasses. "To Viola, the next big name in graphic design," he says.

"Thanks, dude."

The band resumes playing. "You wanna dance?" he shouts in my ear.

His closeness causes a new thought to zap me like an electric bolt. What better revenge against Anthony than to have sex with another man? I take a silent vow to have a mind-blowing one-night-stand with the man of my dreams, assuming he's agreeable, of course. At this moment, Freddie looks like the perfect prospect. He's handsome and well-muscled and doesn't appear to be the type to complicate my life with an emotional attachment.

"I love to dance," I tell him. I'm not expecting much out of his dancing skills, so it blows me away when he leaves his jacket on a chair, takes my hand, and swings us around the dance floor like we're the twenty-first century's answer to Patrick Swayze and Jennifer Grey. I'm decent enough to follow his lead for the most part, though I've never been in such confident hands as his before. I feel like I struck the dancing jackpot tonight. A few times he breaks from me to partner with other women he knows, and I wait impatiently for him to return and pull me out on the floor again.

Jackie comes up to me. "You and Freddie make a great dance team."

"Is he married?" I ask.

"Don't you have a husband?"

"Only one I'd prefer not to see again. Don't tell anyone, but I'm looking for a brief fling while I'm here."

"For the record, Freddie has one too."

"One what?"

"A husband. The man can't dance though, and Freddie thinks women make better partners anyway."

My spirit sinks. I thought it would be easy to invite him back to the house tonight and make quick work of my revenge pledge. It's likely too late now to find another promising prospect, considering I've been hitting the martinis pretty hard. A wave of dizziness comes over me while I watch Freddie twirl his partner. Overheated and stifled by the indoor air, I push through the crowd that's grown considerably since the band started to play. Outside, I gulp fresh oxygen and allow the sensation of frigid wind blowing over my flushed cheeks to revive me.

The soothing sound of waves breaking on the shore across the street draws my gaze. A full moon rises in the east, casting an orange glow over the rippling sea. Its beauty calls out to the artist in me, urging my steps across the street and parking lot. I glide like a specter down the stairs leading to the sand, where the insane idea to do a polar plunge fills me. I yank off my boots to get started.

Mom's voice fills my head. *What are you doing? It's January! You can't go in the water. At your age, you'll get a heart attack.*

Anthony's voice mingles with hers. *Cut the shit, Vi. You're being irrational. Don't go in the water. I order you not to.*

Driven by the compulsion to defy them, I throw off my coat and pull off my pants. It must be the alcohol, but I barely notice the cold. My shirt comes next, leaving me only my bra and panties, which anyway are the exact components of a woman's bathing suit.

With my first steps into the water, a powerful sensation overwhelms me. *I can do anything.* Though the cold robs me of breath, I keep going. The icy water slices across my waist as I prepare to dive.

But first two powerful hands grip my shoulders from behind.

9

THE THWARTED RESCUE

"L**et me go!**" I scream.

"Hey, hey, I just want to help," the man says. "You don't have to do this."

I struggle to free myself, unsuccessfully. "Take your hands off me!"

"Only if you promise not to hurt yourself."

"I'm just doing a polar plunge." The words sound funny as my teeth are now chattering. "Not drowning myself!"

"You swear?"

"Yes, goddammit!"

He releases me. "Okay then, go ahead."

But the moment of divine grace has passed and bitter cold overwhelms me. Each touch of the waves feels like knives stabbing into me. "You ruined it!" I spin around and see the interloper for the first time.

I don't know what I was expecting but it certainly wasn't this man, who reminds me of a sixty-ish Sean Connery with the moon highlighting his hawklike nose, strong chin, and gray whiskers. His dark eyes have a penetrating gaze that warms my insides despite my frozen outer shell. I'm suddenly aware how little clothing I have on.

"No really, go ahead and plunge. I didn't mean to ruin your fun."

I can tell he's just messing with me now. "You're obviously cold. I'm getting out for your sake," I say, heading to shore, praying he isn't eyeing my ass through the wet, clingy underwear.

He reaches my coat where I flung it before I do, and wraps it around me like he's my fairy knight in shining armor.

"Who are you?" I say in wonder.

"I was walking on the beach. The way you went toward the ocean, you were so intent, it was like you were on a mission. I wanted to be sure you were all right."

"I might've had a little too much to drink."

"We've all been there," he says.

I pick up my remaining clothing. "I'm not like this normally."

"Okay."

"Wait, you say that like you don't believe me."

"I don't know anything about you."

"That's right, you don't. If you knew anything about me, you'd understand why tonight was *fuck it* night."

He gives me a curious glance before putting on the socks and winter boots he left on the beach. "I've got a little time until my soaked pants freeze up and turn me into the Tin Man. Want to tell me?"

I have an urge to shout, *because my mother slept with my husband*, but I restrain myself. "It's complicated."

"Vi!" Jackie yells from the top of the steps before racing down them toward me. "Vi, what the hell?"

"I'm fine. Just got the wild notion to do a polar plunge."

"Oh thank god! I thought you must've lost your mind."

Only a New Englander would not take the desire to do a polar plunge as proof of insanity.

She has my boots and stockings. "These wouldn't be yours, would they?" Like a true friend, she helps stabilize me while I put them on.

I turn back to thank the man for being a good Samaritan, and to see if I can get his number as a possible future one-exquisite-night-of-carnal-pleasure prospect because doing anything tonight is now out of the question what with my being frozen and soaked and drunk. But my savior is gone. *What the ferk?* Whirling around, I check all directions, including the sea. Could he have been a merman who got his legs when he came out of the water? "Did you see where that man went?" I ask Jackie.

"What man?" she says.

10

FOOD ANTHONY HATES

I wake at eleven to fifteen texts from Anthony that say *Call me right away.*

I don't call him right away. He'll be lucky if I ever call him again.

I make coffee, of course. And toast. I eat by the window, watching delicate flakes of snow floating downward. Have I mentioned that snow and the sea are my two favorite outdoor things in the whole wide world? I wonder again why I ever left this place.

Twenty minutes later, two buzzkills occur simultaneously when the snow stops falling and a call comes in from Anthony. I stare at his name on the screen, wondering if it might be possible never to speak to him again. Alas, no. Even if I could divorce him instantly, there would need to be conversations.

I text him a few minutes after not answering his call. *Can't talk right now.*

Where are you? is his instant reply.

Home. I'm fine.

Why didn't you answer my texts?

Because you screwed my mom, is what I'm thinking. *I was out with a friend last night.*

Should I be worried? he asks.

Told you I'm fine. I decide to turn things around on him. *You coming to Mom's viewing?*

This time his response takes a minute. Then, *Can't make it. Have to work on the book. Deadline coming up.*

Funny, he used to tell me deadlines were amorphous things. Of course, I knew he wouldn't be coming, because that would mean he'd have to help with all the post-death jobs that need doing, not to mention provide a shoulder for me to cry on. It still shocks me that after all the years of Mom being his biggest supporter, starting from the day she went to his stupid lecture and then followed him home and fornicated him... that after all this, he's not willing to take two days to fly here and wish her a safe journey to wherever she might be going if there's an afterlife.

Gotta run, I text. *Appt with the lawyer.*

Immediately after, I text Max, giving the date and time for the visitation and asking if she still plans to come. Without waiting for a response—sometimes she takes hours—I head out to the downtown market to replenish Mom's coffee supply. Unlike my normal shopping, when I'm hyper-organized and only buy items on my list, I take my time strolling down each aisle, scanning the shelves for anything that strikes my fancy. In the produce section, I select eggplant, beets, bananas, and arugula to complement the ingredients I have at home already. It isn't till I pick up hazelnuts in the next aisle that I realize it's all food Anthony would never eat. I cackle to myself as I make food-Anthony-hates the theme of my shopping expedition, tossing cornbread mix, canned pineapple, Boston baked beans, cottage cheese, and a box of Lucky Charms into my cart. Lastly, I snag a bag of doggie treats to remind myself that I could, if I insisted, adopt a little pup and bring her back to

California. I would relish the look of dread on Anthony's face as I walked off the plane with a high-spirited furball wrapped in my arms.

Back home I put away the groceries and receive a text from Max. *Can't make it to the visitation. Have to work that night.*

It's okay. We're going to do a celebration of her life in the summer, I text back.

Magnificent! I'll help you plan it

Returning to the family room with tea, I get out Mom's *death plans* which were underneath her horrible confession in the drawer by her seat. I sit on the couch—never Mom's chair— and dial the first number on her list of friends. After three rings, a woman with a tremulous voice answers.

"Hello, is this Hannah?" I rush on without waiting for a reply, afraid she'll think I'm a telemarketer and hang up. "This is Viola, Rosemary Sagewood's daughter."

"Viola. I remember you from when you were little. I'm sorry for your loss, sweetie."

Word spreads fast in this small town. "Thank you. How did you find out?"

"My friend Jane was at Primavera's."

"Is that the restaurant where Mom died? Was Jane with her?"

"Yes... and no. Jane wasn't with your mother. She was there with her husband."

"Did she see who was with Mom? She couldn't have gone alone. Her car is here." And she didn't know how to use rideshare apps.

"She was with a gentleman but Jane didn't recognize him."

"A gentleman?" I scan the list in front of me. There are two men's names.

"That's right."

"Do you have any idea who he might have been?"

"No, dear. Do you know how caring and thoughtful your

mother was? Last week when I had the flu, she dropped off a quiche. I'm going to miss her very much."

We hang up after I tell her about the visitation, and the remaining calls keep me busy through the late afternoon. Every one of her friends already knows she has passed, a testament to our town's gossip network. Some want to talk endlessly about her, while others are more perfunctory. I suppose people over the age of eighty have to harden their reactions so as not to be overwhelmed by all the news of illness and death.

Mom's voice arises from her chair: *My friends are dropping like flies.*

I speak to the two men on the list, who both deny being at the restaurant with Mom when she died. One tells me in a tone of heavy betrayal that he no longer drives because his kids took away his license. I briefly wonder how they managed it before reminding myself of the silver lining of Mom's passing—her driving is no longer a danger to anyone.

With no more excuses to delay my visit to the funeral home, I head off again in Mom's car. The trembling starts as I pull into the parking lot and the reality of seeing my deceased mother sinks in. I hug and rock myself for several moments before lugging myself from the car into the building, bearing the emotionally heavy weight of her *death outfit* as Mom called it. On seeing me, Billy the funeral director springs from his seat to whisk away my burden and offer condolences.

I thank him. He's the little brother of Catherine, my best friend in elementary school, and he still wears that same hangdog look he had when she yelled at him for playing with her dollhouse.

"Is she ready for me?" As I say this I wonder if *I* am ready for her.

"This way." When he notices me swaying, he grasps my elbow firmly and escorts me into the private viewing area, where Mom lies on a flat surface wearing a white nightgown with a sheet pulled up over her lower half and her hands folded over her chest.

"She's been prepared, except for her clothes. Let me get you a seat," he says.

I collapse into the chair he places beside my mother, but wait until he tiptoes from the room before taking a long, hard look at her. They did a passable job making her appear much as she did in life, though the blush on her cheeks can't disguise the truth that blood no longer flows through her veins.

It's evident that in the short time since I last saw her, my mother had her hair and nails done. Since Mom was very particular about her appearance, she would've made salon and manicure appointments to precede her dinner out with the man who has yet to be identified. It's also true that if she had a premonition she was going to die within the week, her first instinct would have been to book her beauty treatments.

Noticing her wedding and engagement rings are missing from her finger, I make a mental note to ask the director for them on my way out.

"I'm here, Mom."

Hello, sweetheart, she says inside my head.

"Don't *sweetheart* me. I read your confession." I've made no progress in stamping out the hot embers of anger and resentment.

You'll feel better if you forgive me.

I scoff. "Fat chance. It's your fault I married Anthony. And doubly your fault I'm still with him now."

Your choice not mine... you loved him.

"I wouldn't have gone on a single date with him if I knew what went on between the two of you."

That's why I didn't tell you.

Heat rushes through me. "I can't bear to look at you right now." I stalk away from her and return to Billy's office.

"Here are the death certificates." He hands me a manila envelope.

"And her effects?"

He appears confused. "Effects?"

"You know, the stuff she had with her when she died. Her clothes, her phone... her rings."

"They didn't send anything over from the hospital. She wasn't wearing any jewelry at all. I assumed they had given them to you there. You'll need to contact them."

11

THE HOPEFUL ROMANTIC

During the night I dream about the man who tried to save me from plunging into the freezing cold ocean. Instead of winter, it's a hot summer day at high tide when he swims up to the back of our deck like he's Michael Phelps in the final heat of a relay. He stops abruptly and shouts out my name while he treads water. A minute later he's flopping his arms and panicking like he no longer has any idea how to swim. I dive off the deck to rescue him—after all, I did earn my lifesaving certificate when I was a teenager—but when I look around in the water, he's gone.

The dream wakes me and gets me thinking about him. Why didn't I get his phone number? It was *fuck it* night, for god's sake. But Jackie distracted me.

I see red whenever I think of Anthony and the skeleton he kept in the closet all these years. I'm still determined to have my own secret liaison with someone yet-to-be-determined but it's going to take longer to arrange than I imagined. I'm simply not the kind of person to sleep with someone random I meet in a bar. There has to be physical attraction and some amount of personal connection to make the act enjoyable to me. Otherwise, I'm just making myself miserable in order to picture how miserable Anthony will be if he ever finds out. My goal should be to give myself the maximum amount of pleasure while imagining Anthony's misery.

My mind wanders to Jackie and Ken. I used to think online dating was for scammers and losers, but I'm not so sure now. How else would someone my age meet anyone remotely compatible? At the bar, I met a gay man and someone nice at the beach who's probably married, except I'll never know because I neglected to get his phone number.

A little voice in my head is egging me on to try it. *Why not?* Before I consider the leap of divorce, I'd like to know if there's a chance of meeting someone who doesn't view women as unpaid manual laborers with benefits. And if I somehow hook up with a hot guy who's not an asshole, I can achieve my dream of a single night of mind-blowing sex beyond anything I can imagine.

Can any man can find me sexually desirable at this age? It's not hard if you've known someone forever and adjusted to the gradual changes in their appearance over the decades. But when you meet them for the first time and they already have a face infested by wrinkles, how do you get past that to appreciate the beauty of the person inside? This is one of many questions I seek to have answered. In the past when I sometimes thought about divorce, I always pictured myself celibate in the aftermath, but Jackie's example has made me wonder if there could be a man out there who would willingly jump into the sack with me.

I settle on the couch in the family room with my laptop to begin my research. The main thing I hope to avoid is hookup sites like Tinder. The whole swiping system seems needlessly cruel, although I'm not sure if the user is aware when they're being rejected. I remember Jackie told me she used thehopeful-romantic dot com. After a brief check of two of the most popular apps, I decide to stick with her choice because I value Jackie's recommendation and I like the positive attitude projected by its name.

First I choose the fake name *Vicki* for my profile, because, you know, there could be swindlers and axe murderers on the site and I don't want to make it easy for them to track me down. Although, let's face it, if they really wanted to find me they could probably use a face recognition app and have my full name, address, net worth, and elementary school transcript with one click of the mouse.

I set my search area to Mom's neighborhood, not because guys are manlier here, as the ghost of Mom suggests from her chair. Obviously I won't be dating back in California with Anthony breathing down my neck. Accessing the photos on my phone, I scan for any of myself that don't make me want to print them out just to tear them into pieces and flush them down the toilet. Unfortunately, all the ones Anthony took of me are like this, because he is the world's suckiest photographer. Honestly, it isn't just me, he could make Julia Roberts look like a baboon.

Eventually I find a few decent photos. One taken by Max when we were out to dinner right after I had my hair colored, and another with me standing beside our persimmon tree.

What's a persimmon tree? Mom asks.

Hmm, good point, no one in Massachusetts has ever seen one. This reminds me photos can be exotic and imply that one is a worldwide traveler. I return to a pose of me with the Golden Gate Bridge in the background, which I rejected earlier for being cliché, and upload it to my page.

Three pictures are enough, I don't need to create the perfect profile. I'm not looking for a lifelong partner, I'm conducting research on the type of men to be found on dating sites plus keeping my options open for a possible sexual liaison. I apply the same lack of effort to writing my profile, which looks like far too much work if I were to do it properly. Instead, I half-ass it and give myself a lower-middle class income to avoid attracting fortune hunters. I write the correct number of kids— one—and grandkids—zero so far.

I'm muttering aloud as I type in my religion and politics, thinking this will help weed out a lot of incompatible dates, when Mom pipes in. *Know who has the same religion and politics as you?*

Dammit, she's right, Anthony does, and look where that got me? I decide to leave those fields blank.

I move on to my favorite foods, films, books, music, and activities because the algorithm probably needs a little help to match me with men who might have something in common with me. I hesitate when asked what kind of relationship I'm looking for.

Escort? Mom offers.

A confident, capable, intensely attractive fuck buddy for one night, is what I'm thinking. But I'm afraid if I admit sex is my goal, my profile will attract a bevy of weirdos. "Friendship and connection with a like-minded man," I say while I write.

Reaching the most important question—whether I'm Single, Married, Divorced, or Widowed—I check the box for Divorced.

Liar, Mom hisses. *Liar, liar, pants on fire.*

I refuse to look at her spectral image. If I tell the truth about being married, I'll attract the worst kind of lowlifes cheating on their wives and girlfriends. I beat away the pesky thought that I will be the exact same kind of low-life when I cheat on my husband. It's different for me, obviously. If any of these cheating husbands can claim their wife slept with their father, I'll give them a pass.

Holding my breath, I launch my profile into the void.

12

THE SEND OFF

In the morning, I try calling the doctor who notified me of Mom's death, but fail to reach a human being on the other end of the line. Eventually I drive over to the hospital and speak to a poker-faced man wearing tinted glasses who works in a shadowy administrative department.

"The triage nurse who dealt with her when the ambulance brought her to the hospital would have been the one to gather her personal items."

"You do triage on dead people?"

"We still had to assign her to a doctor who would verify death."

"Can I speak to her?"

He looks at his computer and grunts. "She's off today."

"You couldn't call her at home?"

He wrinkles his nose like the question smells bad. "I'll leave a note for her to call you when she's back," he says.

I decide not to press him further. I don't want to risk losing his tenuous cooperation. It won't kill my mother to wait another twenty-four hours.

.   .   .

BACK AT MOM'S HOUSE, I prepare for her visitation, set for 1:00 to 4:00 pm. After showering, styling my hair, and pairing a lavender blouse with a black skirt, I slide into Mom's beautiful wool coat and stylish boots again—now fully dried out and de-sanded following my beach escapade—before setting out.

I discuss a few details with the director before joining her corpse in the viewing room to await our guests. She almost looks like you could poke her awake, lying there in her red blazer, Cadillac pin, black pants, and killer high heels that she could not wear in real life.

"I'm back, Mom," I say. "But I still haven't forgiven you."

You can pretend, can't you? All my friends will be here.

"I wonder what they'd say if they knew."

Everybody's got dirty laundry.

"I don't. I wish I did."

Noises approach behind me and I spin around. Mary Ellen, a longtime friend of Mom's, creeps toward us using a walker. I don't care if she heard me talking, I'm sick of lies and pretenses.

"Your mother was a generous woman," Mary Ellen tells me. "I remember the time she sold me a gorgeous dress for fifty percent off after my husband got laid off."

"Her markups were generally sixty percent, though," I say.

As more people arrive, I withdraw to a chair by the wall. I'm not eager to hear their praise of her. This viewing might have been a bad idea.

Most of the visitors insist on approaching me to express their condolences. "One time I got a flat, and who should pull up but your mother," says a woman I don't recognize. "She was dressed like she was headed to a photo shoot, but it didn't stop her from changing that tire in record time."

"She liked playing the hero. She fed on people's admiration," I say.

The accolades keep flowing.

"No one could beat her at gin rummy."

"That's because she cheated."

"She was so proud of you. Always talking up your accomplishments. You were lucky to have a mother like her."

"That's what *she* always said."

"She's with the angels now." This from her old friend Denise.

"The dark angels," I mutter.

I get up to use the restroom, and when I return, Mary Ellen and Denise are hovering over Mom. "Her hands look so pale," Mary Ellen says.

"You do know she's dead," says Denise.

"Yes, but her cheeks are rosier than ever."

"Maybe she's blushing, listening to us talking about her."

"She looks taller than I remember."

"It's the shoes. Look at those stilettos."

"Recipe for a hip replacement." Mary Ellen shakes her head.

"She won't need one where she's going."

Laughter gurgles up inside me. I have to cover my mouth and look away, which is when I see a man entering by himself. He walks over to the display table and sets down a bouquet of lilies. Dressed casually in jeans, a parka, and a Boston Celtics cap, he has regular features and a close beard. Some of the women glance his way but no one appears to recognize him. He avoids making eye contact with anyone. I wonder if he could be Mom's date the night she died, but he seems way too young, probably mid-fifties. Still, just in case, I approach him. "Thank you for the flowers. Lilies were my mother's favorites."

His eyes dart in my direction. "Sorry for your loss." He turns away.

"Wait." I'm convinced now there's something suspicious about him. "How do you know her?"

"Excuse me, I'm in a hurry." He increases his pace toward the door.

"What's your name?"

He doesn't answer as he rushes out past a woman arriving in a wheelchair. As I attempt to follow him, the woman blocks me at the doorway. "You must be Viola," she says.

"Yes, thank you for coming." I ignore the rest of what she says while I struggle to maneuver around her. "I'll be back in a minute," I tell her.

But when I get outside, the man is nowhere to be seen. I hurry around the corner of the building in time to spot a metallic silver Mercedes sedan backing out of a space in the lot. Jogging toward it, I notice a ding on the right back fender, and a Red Sox decal—literally a pair of red socks—on the bottom left of the rear window. The car turns onto the street before I can read the license, and speeds away.

Just as I'm contemplating getting in the Cadillac and giving chase, a scream comes from inside the funeral home.

Oh lord, what now?

Part of me wants to keep running and never return. But the other part, the responsible side, makes me stop, turn around, and return to the funeral home to face whatever emergency has occurred.

"She's alive!" This apparently from the screamer.

As I race toward where Mom's friends are crowded around her, I wonder if other people can hear her speaking now.

"For goodness sake, Julie. Ansley bumped the table with the wheelchair," Denise explains. "And her hand dropped down."

Billy the funeral director joins us. "Everything all right, ladies?"

"This wheelchair is out of control," Ansley says. "I apologize for it."

"She opened her mouth!" Julie points at Mom's lips, which have indeed come open. "I swear she's alive!"

The fact that she looks like she's smiling is the tipping point that sends me hurtling over the edge. Laughter erupts out of me, fueled by the words echoing inside my head, and there's nothing I can do to stop it. *Her hands look so pale... You do know she's dead... She's alive!* This one reminds me of the ridiculous *Bride of Frankenstein* movie. I could swear Mom is laughing right along with me.

"Viola's hysterical," Mary Ellen says.

"Poor thing," Denise says. "Her husband's not here." She lowers her voice. "I hear he has cancer."

This rumor that comes out of nowhere makes me laugh harder.

"Oh no, what was his name? Tony? The MIT professor? Rosemary was wild about him."

Mary Ellen having no idea how close she is to the truth just makes the whole thing funnier. Tears course down my cheeks.

Billy is occupied trying to restore Mom to her serene pose. Ansley in her wheelchair reaches up and pats my back. "Now, now, dear. Everything will be all right."

When I glance down at her, she says "Julie is..." and rolls her finger pointing at her head in the universal *she's cuckoo* signal.

Now I'm bent over double, out of control.

Finished with arranging Mom, Billy comes over to me, puts a firm hand on my back, and leads me out of the room. I go into the ladies and lean over the counter staring at the wild woman in the mirror. I look like Lucille Ball midway through any *I Love Lucy* episode. After several more minutes, my laughter dissolves into hiccups. I throw water on my face and take deep breaths.

By the time I return to the visitation room, everyone has gone. Footsteps approach behind me. "You okay?" Billy asks.

"Yeah. Sorry for that."

"Emotions are high. It happens all the time."

Nice of him to say, but I doubt it. "Can I have a few minutes alone with her?"

"Of course."

I wander over to the lilies, and feeling a stab of excitement on seeing the man left a card, I tear it open to find this message: "I will love you forever. -H."

There is no other identifying information, not even anything to show where the flowers were purchased. If he was Mom's missing date, he's undoubtedly a con artist. On the other hand, would a con artist drop off flowers and a beautiful message at the risk of being caught?

I approach my mother, thinking how she'll be reduced to ashes in just a few hours, and place my hand over her nose and mouth, checking for breath. "You aren't really alive, are you?"

Only for you, baby.

"That guy who came... was it him?"

Don't know what you're talking about.

"The man at the restaurant."

She doesn't answer, just lies there looking like an elderly heavenly angel. I adjust a fold in her jacket. "I want to forgive you, Mom."

You will. You can't help yourself.

I sob. "You ruined my life. You could've confessed years ago and it would've been the excuse I needed to leave that bastard."

You always forgive him. You would've forgiven him then too. It has nothing to do with me.

"Stop saying what I don't want to hear."

Her silence while I weep brings a tightness to my chest. "You can't leave me. How will I live without you?"

She doesn't tell me.

13

THE FISH

In the morning I'm staring at the ocean sipping my coffee when someone knocks at the door, surprising me.

Maybe it's Mom's mystery date. My nerves prickling, I peek out the side window, but it's just Jackie. When I let her in, she hugs me tight. "I'm sorry I didn't go to the visitation. It's not personal. I just can't stand looking at dead bodies."

"Sure, we've all got our thing. Don't worry about it. Can I get you some coffee?"

"Already had two cups." She sweeps past me into Mom's designer kitchen. "I forgot how amazing this house is." She scrutinizes the windows, floor, cabinets, and countertops before pausing at a small painting on the wall. "Did you do this?"

"Yup."

"It's good."

Funny how the brain filters out anything you grow accustomed to seeing, just like those floaters that occasionally explode across my vision. Every time I worry it's going to permanently block my eyesight, then three weeks later, I kind of know it's still there but I barely see it. My painting hanging on Mom's wall is like this—I have to walk over next to Jackie to check it out.

I remember painting it now, Mom in her Hatteras-blue Cadillac Convertible with the top down. I did it in my twenties, sometime after the used car lot disaster when the salesman saved me from getting struck by the killer car. Mom is wearing a scarf and sunglasses, and she bears a surprising resemblance to Louise of the movie *Thelma and Louise*, considering the movie didn't come out till a couple years later. Just as in the eventual movie, Mom's car appears like it's flying through the air, with the back third of the vehicle dissolving into bare canvas. At my mother's request, I angled her Cadillac in an upward direction like she's heading to heaven. I should've brought this to the viewing to give Mary Ellen and Denise more food for speculation.

"Are you still doing original paintings?" Jackie asks.

"No. I'm working on digital art design. There's more money in it."

"How do you know if you haven't tried? It's a friggin' waste to have you designing ads for tune-up shops instead of creating real art, which I can see by this you're perfectly capable of doing."

It occurs to me, both Anthony and Mom discouraged me from trying to make a career out of my art. Mom had a ridiculous saying that *the 'ar' in starving stands for artist.* Anthony's refrain was *no one buys art, unless their last name is Buffet or Gates.* Actually, neither of these men are known for their art collections.

"I do the framing for some artists who belong to the Windset Art Society," Jackie says. "They have their Winter Arts Festival coming up. It's a big fundraiser for them, at the Thornwood House a few weeks from now. Have you ever been there?"

I shake my head.

"It's a beautifully restored historic home, built in 1689, with a giant stone fireplace. It's the definition of cozy in the winter. The society puts on a juried show and there's an opening night gala. You should submit something."

"I don't have anything to submit."

"Well paint something! I have influence there; they'll consider your work even if it's past the deadline. The Winter Festival is a big deal around here, and it attracts the folks with money. It wouldn't hurt you to give it a try."

Jackie continues her examination of everything, spotting a wedding photo of me and Anthony on a side shelf. She picks it up to scrutinize it. "Aww, look at the two of you. He's very handsome."

I snatch it away from her and shove it in a drawer. "I don't want to look at that."

"Why do I get the feeling there's something you're not telling me about your marriage?"

I swear, the need to share my condemnation of Mom and Anthony causes actual pain in my esophagus. "Okay, I'll tell you if you promise to keep it to yourself."

"I will."

I take a deep breath. "My mother slept with my husband."

"WHAT? Oh my god, that's terrible! Why are you still with him?"

I suddenly feel the need to justify the act. "It was before I met him. Just a one-night stand."

"*Just* a one-night stand between your mother and husband? That's still unforgivable, especially if they kept it secret from you."

"Mom left me a deathbed confession."

"So for what, like forty years, no one told you?"

"Right."

"That's grounds for leaving him penniless in the divorce. Does he know you know?"

"I'm waiting for precisely the right moment to let that out."

"I bet *he's* not leaving you a deathbed confession. Why did your mother ever let you marry him?"

"Despite what happened, she thought he was prime husband material for me."

"I knew your mother wasn't normal but I never could've imagined this. What are you going to do?"

"I'll show you." I fetch my laptop from the other room and open it up. "I signed up for online dating."

"You go, girl. So you filed for divorce?"

"I'm seeing who's out there first. Want to check my matches with me?"

"Hell yeah."

I get onto the dating site. "Have a seat." Excitement bubbles up inside me.

Jackie takes the counter stool next to mine as I scroll through photos. "What's with these guys with no pictures?" I'm not sure how much time she spent online dating, but compared to me, she's the expert.

"Either laziness or low self-esteem," she says. "But they should know any photo is bound to be better than what we imagine."

"I'm picturing Frankenstein."

"The creature from the Black Lagoon," she says.

"Gollum."

"Alien."

"I almost want to meet them now, just to see," I say.

We scan through the next dozen. "Gotta love the bathroom mirror selfies," Jackie says.

"A reliable way to eliminate yourself from the dating pool."

I peer ahead at the next photo and laugh out loud. "This guy cut his wife out of the photo. Except her fingers on his shoulder."

"If he's too lazy to take a new picture minus his ex, don't expect him to ever wash a dish or pick up his dirty underwear."

As we continue through the list, I pause at the third guy we've seen holding up a large fish he caught. "What are your thoughts?" I ask Jackie.

"Compared to that fish, his penis is bound to be a letdown."

"I want to know how come all the bald men wear baseball caps," I say.

"Better than a toupee."

"Sure, but why not try something different? Like an Indiana Jones hat. Or a Peaky Blinders cap."

"I love the hats men wore in the 50s."

"Mm, I remember my father's." I get a mental image of him coming home from work wearing his hat, a trench coat, and patent leather shoes.

Moving on, we discover another trend. "These guys with old black & white photos have got hair styles and clothing from the 1980s."

"Who needs new pictures? I'm sure they haven't changed a bit since then," Jackie says. "Have we found anyone you'd like to reach out to?"

"I do like the ones posing with their dogs or cats. I don't suppose you have an adorable pet I can borrow for a selfie?"

"Dexter my lizard would love to sit in your lap."

Unsure if she's serious, I let the subject drop.

"Wait, here he is. This is the one. He looks like Bradley Cooper," I say.

"Kiddo, look closer. That *is* Bradley Cooper."

"All the better. I should let him know I'm available right now." I click to examine his page. "Do you think he set up this profile himself? It has nothing in it."

"All the most gorgeous men have blank pages. Their looks speak for themselves. No one cares about their personalities."

The computer dings.

"Hey look, I have a message already." I click on the man's

profile. "This one looks like Colin Firth. Colin says I have a beautiful smile."

Jackie snorts. "I know it seems like a wasteland, but if you're patient, you just might find someone you like." She gets up. "I have to run."

"Were you serious that I should submit to the arts festival?"

"Never more so."

"I'll see what I can do."

14

THE HUSBAND

I get a call from the funeral home informing me Mom's ashes are ready for pickup. I need to bring her home, though my insides are churning at the thought of it.

When I arrive, Billy ushers me into what looks like a cremated remains storage area and picks up the beautiful mahogany box I selected for her. Before I can stop him, he opens the top to show me what's inside, making me screech at the sight of her remains. "What are those bones?!" There are two fragments.

He closes the box quickly. "Sometimes that happens."

"The ashes look weird. They're all gray. Are you sure that's my mother?" I thought they would look like ashes in a fireplace. These are clumpy strands, like they've been stored in a spider-infested crypt for thousands of years.

"Positively. The bones make the ashes look like that. I'm sorry I opened it. Most people like to verify their loved one is inside."

I restrain myself from commenting that it could be the remains of a rabid raccoon for all I can tell. I'm taking his word that it's my mother, and I'd rather not see evidence of an incomplete cremation, thank you very much. My hands are shaking as he holds out the box. I'm petrified I'll drop it, the lid will come open again, and the contents will fly out and spread across the room. I wonder if I breathe in her ashes, will I always have a part of her inside me? By that token, Billy will own a part of her too.

When I accept the box from him, I discover its other surprising quality. "It's heavy!"

"That's because of—"

"—the bones," I finish for him.

"Do you need help?" he asks.

Desperately. "No, thank you." I grab a few breaths to steady myself and pray I make it to the car without tripping. When we get to the passenger seat, I sigh in relief and wonder if I should belt her in. Given the low height of the box, it isn't really possible, otherwise I would. "We're taking you home, Mom." A tear slips down my cheek.

Back at the house, I don't place her on her chair because I spend a good deal of time in that room and it will be sad having a constant reminder of her being dead. Instead, I lay her down on her bed and sit with her for a moment. I touch the smooth wood and regret my decision not to engrave her name on it. When Billy asked, I thought it wasn't necessary because I plan to release her ashes into the ocean as soon as weather permits. But after that, I could engrave this box that she occupied temporarily and use it to store something of hers.

I glance around her room as my thoughts migrate to the question of what I need to do next. The answer, of course, is to go through Mom's stuff. I have to make tough decisions regarding what to keep, what to give to friends and family, what to sell, and what to bring to the charity shop. Anthony will naturally expect me to complete this job as quickly as possible so that I can rush back to California and take care of him.

My mind revolts against this idea, and turns to the one that excites me—creating a new painting. I check to see if there might be any art supplies hidden away in my old bedroom, but Mom did a thorough job of chucking all my remaining personal belongings the second I walked out the front door headed for college. Now my bedroom is a generic guest room like any Airbnb with a smashing view of the ocean. Still, I stare at the cedar chest at the foot of the bed, recalling the easel, acrylic paints, canvases, brushes, and palette that she gave away without asking me, thinking old resentments die hard.

No matter. I spend the remainder of the day at the local arts and crafts store, loading up on all the colors and supplies I could possibly need for whatever I choose to paint. I'm practically giddy by the time I roll my cart up to the cashier.

"Taking a painting class?" she asks.

"I know how to paint. I just haven't done it for years. I can't wait to get started," I gush.

AFTER TOSSING my new purchases in the family room, I throw together an omelet for dinner, but as soon as I sit down, my phone rings. Normally I ignore unidentified numbers, especially when eating, but these days I'm answering everything in case it has anything to do with Mom.

"This is Karen Santos," the woman says. "I was the intake nurse when your mother arrived at the hospital. Sorry for your loss."

"Thank you. Do you have her effects?"

"I gave them to your father," she says. "Didn't he tell you?"

My mouth drops open. I take a minute to find words.

"You still there?" she asks.

"My father is dead."

"Oh my god, did you lose him too? I've heard about couples who die at the same time, like they can't bear to live without each other."

"No, he died years ago."

"So the man was your stepfather?"

"I don't have a stepfather. He must've been a friend of hers," I say.

"But he said he was her husband."

"What?"

"He told me he was her husband."

"That's not possible. Maybe you didn't hear him right."

"I'm sure he said it. He seemed very distraught. He came with her in the ambulance."

"You're positive?"

"Absolutely. I remember thinking how sad it was he lost her."

My mind is reeling. "Did he say his name? Did you check his ID?"

"The EMT also called him her husband. There was no reason to doubt it. He looked around the same age."

If so, this was not the man who brought the lilies to Mom's viewing. "Can you give me a description?" I ask.

"I don't know. White hair. Medium height. A stomach bulge."

She has just described eighty percent of senior men. "What exactly did you give him?"

"Her purse. Her phone. And her wedding rings."

Who in their right mind would marry an eighty-nine-year old? No one legitimate. Even if they could ignore her skin hanging off her body like melted wax, or her arthritic hands curled up like gnarled tree roots, would they really want to put time into a relationship that could quickly devolve into three years of nursing home visits followed by death? Besides, someone legit would've come forward and returned her stuff.

If she did marry someone, he's guaranteed to be a crook.

She wasn't wealthy, or even close to it, but she was comfortably off. It makes me sick the way scammers take advantage of older folks who might have dementia. Mom was showing signs of decreased mental capacity. I suppose it's possible he tricked her into marrying him, but if she did, there ought to be a marriage certificate somewhere in the house. I begin the search immediately, checking documents lying on counters, desks, and chairs, filed in drawers, and haphazardly abandoned inside cupboards. I find plenty of annoying crap like unpaid bills I'll have to deal with at some point, but no certificate or anything else pointing to a new husband, boyfriend, or casual date in her life.

When I've run out of places to look, I make a phone call.

"Windset Police Department," the operator says.

"I, um, would like to speak to a detective."

A few moments later, I'm talking to Detective Dempsey. "I'm calling to report a..." What was I calling to report? "Um, my elderly mother was the victim of a swindler." I spew out Mom's story.

"Did-she-and-the-man-claiming-to-be-her-husband-meet-on-a-dating-app?" The detective speaks so fast, his whole sentence sounds like one very long word.

"She was eighty-nine-years-old, Detective."

"My-father's-eighty-two-and-he-just-gave-his-eighty-five-year-old-girlfriend-a-ring-like-they're-sweet-sixteen.   Fastest-growing-group-of-online-daters? Codgers."

"Okay, well can you help me find him?"

"Do-you-know-his-name? His-address?"

"I don't know anything about him."

"Okay-then-come-to-the-station-and-fill-out-a-report."

I cup the receiver and turn to Mom's chair. "Could this detective be an AI?"

I heard they're replacing writers, why not cops?

"Can't I give you the information over the phone?" I say to the detective.

"No-we-need-you-to-file-a-report. Have-a-nice-evening."

When he hangs up, I turn to Mom's chair. "What on earth did you get yourself into?"

We won't know till you file the report.

15

FIRST CONTACT

For the last week, I've mostly avoided speaking to Anthony with the excuse that I'm neck-deep in issues related to Mom's estate. Actually, all I've done is cancel her credit cards to make sure whoever took her purse is not syphoning off her funds. Aside from that, I'm spending my time painting and occasionally checking my matches on thehopeful-romantic.

I'm feeling bad for my snarky thoughts regarding the men on the dating app. It's insanely difficult putting yourself out there, trying so hard to look and sound like the best version of you. Or for those of us with low self-esteem, aspiring to be the best version of a better person than you. The whole experience could make even the most stalwart soul feel insecure. Now when I look back at my own responses, it's like reading something written by a stranger.

Today I see another scam-level handsome dude, and I'm about to dismiss him when it strikes me I've seen him somewhere before. At first I think he must be an actor in one of the forgettable thriller series I've been watching lately on the streaming channels. Then, *ding ding ding*, I remember who he is

—the man who saved me from an ill-advised dunk in the bone-chilling sea.

"Is this kismet, Mom?" She was the expert on signs and omens.

My mother makes a scoffing sound. I know she's reluctant to encourage me for Anthony's sake. "It's a pretty big coincidence that this man who risked his own, um, comfort, to prevent me from possibly killing myself has now shown up as a recommended match for me. It's got to be a sign."

It's only a sign that you're in over your head.

"Admit it, it's a sign. And what about the fact that he's single?"

So you believe what he says about himself?

"Why would he lie?"

Why would you?

"Stop bothering me with logic."

His name is Michael; it suits him. In one of his photos, he's at the helm of a sailboat—without fish, I notice with relief. In another, he's tilling an enormous garden—that's a bit different for a man, unless his profession is landscaping. The third photo shows him stretched out on a couch facing a fireplace with a beautiful gray tiger cat curled in his lap. Kudos to him for recognizing the appeal of a cuddly animal.

A year older than me, he still works as a building contractor. He says he's planning on fixing up his boat and doing some sailing in his free time. Although this has nothing to do with our possibly meeting up for one night of delicious love-making, it excites me that he could be very handy around the house. I've always wished for a man who could fix things, unlike Anthony who refuses to even try to fix things. However, Michael sounds unrealistically perfect. If I hadn't actually met him, I might think he was fake. Is it possible a scammer is using the man's photo?

His profile has some gems in it, though. "I've had a lot, and

I've had a little, but I'm content with either." A man with experience of life's ups and downs. He sounds real. And deep. He mentions the loves and the heartbreaks he's experienced. He's looking for a new partner to share his life, but he's not cloying or condescending about it. A simple statement from a man who knows what he wants.

I'm going to ignore Mom's insinuation that Michael is a big fat liar like me, and assume he's telling the truth about being divorced. In any case, it isn't my problem if he's straying in his marriage. At the moment I'm not looking for anything long term. However if I was, I would be happy he has just two sons and one granddaughter. I would want to be with someone who has the experience of children, but not an army of them, clamoring for babysitting help from the grandparents.

Halfway through his description, I come to this line: 😊 *Are you still here?* Then a little further, *I can't believe you're still reading this* 👀. And at the very end of the profile: 😮 *Gasp, send help, drowning in a sea of words...*

I'm drowning in a sea of infatuation for this man when his *drowning* comment knocks me back into reality. Michael has seen me drunk, half-naked, and worst of all, ungrateful. He plowed into the ocean like he was Jack handing over the entire piece of Titanic flotsam to Rose, and I didn't even have the courtesy to thank him. Actually, I can't recall her thanking Jack either.

The last person Michael would want to hear from is me. I snap my laptop shut and return to my priority—creating a masterpiece in time for the art show.

AFTER SPENDING several hours at my canvas, the dating app informs me I have a new message from a man named Larry. He's attractive and ten years younger than me. He's also proudly bald—no cap!—and with his dark skin he really rocks the look. Larry used to be employed as an investment banker, and has been working as a voice-over actor for the last three years.

The man looks fit, particularly as he crosses the finish line of the Boston marathon. He has an adorable Jack Russell Terrier named Jilly, who is in his arms or walking by his side in every photo except the marathon, where presumably dogs aren't allowed. This could be the one: he's physically attractive, his career as a voice-over actor could provide interesting conversation to break the ice before jumping into bed with him, and his devotion to his pup is practically proof he isn't a serial killer. According to the shows I watch, they get their start by torturing animals at a young age.

His message is short and may or may not have been written by an AI: *I like your profile. Are you open to a phone conversation? I find it hard to get to know someone by email.*

It seems to me if he were an AI, he'd prefer email. He also scores points for not saying, *I love your smile.* "Should I talk to him, Mom?"

He's too young for you.

"That didn't stop you from hooking up with Anthony."

Yes, but I looked ten years younger than my age.

"There were twenty years between you."

We met in the middle. Anthony looked ten years older than he was.

"Sure, Mom. I think this will be a good test for me. Why not? I deserve a hot young lover."

An hour later we're on the phone. Larry puts it on speaker so his dog Jilly can participate too, and when Jilly speaks, he makes her sound a lot like Elmo from Sesame Street. Larry himself could be mistaken for Fozzie the Bear muppet, but I'm uncertain if that's something he puts on for comic effect, or his actual voice.

"Hi Vicki," Jilly the dog says using my fake online profile

name. "You look like a nice lady! Would you like to come for a walk with me sometime?"

"Um, that sounds like fun. Larry, would you be coming too?" I'm wondering if he plans to use me as a free dog-walker.

"Of course!" Everything he and Jilly say ends with an exclamation point. "Do you have a dog, Vicki?!"

"I'm afraid not. I do love them though."

"That's good because Larry and I do everything together!" Jilly says.

"Which one of you is smarter?"

"Me!" Larry says in his Jilly-Elmo voice. "I know a lot more than he does!"

Five more minutes of this and I would be ready to cut off Larry's tongue. Jilly would thank me for it.

"My hamburger is burning up!" I shout, matching their volume. "It was nice talking to you!" I hang up and block Larry's number.

I barely have time to use the bathroom before my phone rings again. I'm excited to see the call is from Max, who sometimes goes many days without communicating.

"I've been dreaming about Grandma," she says. "I miss her so much."

It's good she's getting enough sleep to have dreams. The poor girl is living in an apartment in Brooklyn with five roommates. The walk-in closet is her bedroom.

"Did lots of people come to the viewing?" she shouts over a siren. She usually calls when she's walking somewhere. I strain to pick out her words from amidst a cacophony of noise—cars honking, brakes squealing, music blasting, and other people shouting.

"Oh yes, the place was filled."

"I hope it wasn't too hard for you. Did you cry a lot, Mom?"

"I did my best to hold it in." Which is more than I can say

for my bout of hysterical laughter. Thank god Max wasn't there to witness that.

"Where did they bury her?"

With everything going on, I've forgotten to fill my daughter in on the details. "She was cremated, darling. Like Granddaddy and your Uncle Keaton."

"I forgot about that! I hate cremation. Grandma should be in a beautiful cemetery where we could go visit her. I wish you had told me!"

"She wanted a sea burial."

"How are we going to visit her there?"

"Rent a boat."

"That's ridiculous," she says. "I'm almost at the subway."

This is code for *we're about to lose our connection.*

"Dad told me you reconnected with an old friend from high school."

Here it comes. Anthony's trying to use her to find out more about my friend. "Yeah, she's great. We're having fun."

"Oh it's a woman? He seems to think it's a guy."

"Did your father ask you to call me?"

"You know how helpless he is. He says everything's piling up at home. Laundry. Dishes. And he's sad. He really misses you."

"I have a lot to do here." I'm staring at my painting when I say this.

"He's afraid he's going to miss his deadline on the book. He wants you to take care of things. Can't you go home and do the rest remotely?"

I can't finish my painting remotely. "No," is all I say.

"Don't blame the messenger, Mom."

"I know you mean well."

"I'm worried about Dad. Something's going on with him, I'm not sure what. Yesterday he texted that he wanted to tell me something. Then today he said he wasn't ready to talk about it. I mean, what the—?"

The line goes dead.

I turn to Mom's chair. "What bullshit."

Anthony?

"Of course, Anthony. 'He wants me to take care of things.' About time the man learned how to plug in a vacuum cleaner." My anger reminds me of my vow to say yes to new adventures. When you say *yes*, things happen, for better or worse. When you say *no*, nothing changes and your life continues down a steady path toward stagnation and death.

I open up the dating app again.

What now?

"I'm going to message the guy from the beach."

Hi Michael, I begin before pausing. "Does it sound like I'm stalking him if I mention our encounter in the water? He might think I got his name there, googled him, and somehow found him on the dating site. On the other hand, if I say nothing and he recognizes me, he'll not only believe I'm stalking him but that I'm trying to hide it."

He won't recognize you. You're a middle-aged woman. People don't see us.

"Mom, you haven't been middle-aged for years. But you have a point. Plus it was dark. Fine, I won't bring it up." I hesitate. "The man is funny. I have to write a funny response to show that I, too, have a sense of humor."

I talk while I'm typing, *Believe it or not, I read your whole profile.*

Mom: *Not funny.*

I try other ideas. *Profiles are a bitch.*

You seem to be a man of many talents, including comedy.

Your profile made me lol!

I delete all of the above.

Mom: *Maybe you could hire someone to write your messages.*

"I'm not giving up yet. How about, *Loved your profile. Please message back if you'd like to start a dialogue.*"

Mom does a robot voice: *Formulate message, begin conversation at the sound of the beep. Beep.*

"I need to sound younger, cooler, hipper. *Dude, your profile is fire.*"

Mom: *Perfect if you were fifteen.*

"What if I'm just honest and direct? *I'm looking for someone who cares for me exactly as I am, who doesn't expect me to work as cook, cleaner, and executive assistant for him, who actually listens to what I have to say, and who is honest and open in his communication with me. I would do my best to treat him the same.*"

Mom: *Oh cry me a river.*

I fiddle with my writing for another ten minutes before reading aloud. *You have that mysterious attractor, a combination of your looks and the way you write about yourself, that makes me think I would enjoy spending time with you.*

Mom: *Forget the words. Just show him a picture of a big fish.*

"What's the female equivalent?"

Mom: *Melons.*

I agonize another hour until I come up with this: *Hi Michael, you had me at "Are you still reading this?" If you'd like to message each other for a bit, I'm in. Viola.*

Mom: *You mean Vicki.*

I change it to my alias. My mouse hovers over the Send button.

Mom: *Don't do it.*

I do it.

THE HARLEY

A week has passed with no response from Michael the beach guy. Whether he isn't replying because he thinks I'm unstable, or because he doesn't find me attractive, it appears a liaison isn't in the cards for us. I need to let it go.

I continue to put off conversations with Anthony, which makes him unhappy but he's trying to finish his book so he lets it go for now. In the evenings during the time I could've spent talking to my husband I check my new matches and messages on the dating app.

Bob, who's a local postmaster, has gotten in touch. The job sounds dull, but he also says he likes hiking and visiting museums. His most beloved place in Boston is the Isabel Stewart Gardner Museum, also a much-loved destination for me. A widower, he's dressed neatly in a light blue button shirt and sometimes a navy jacket in all his photos. No baseball caps or T-shirts for this slender man with silky white hair and a salt-and-pepper mustache. I won't be certain till I meet him in person, but it's possible I could be attracted to him.

However the thing that jumps out at me in his profile is that he rides a Harley motorcycle. A few days ago during a break from my painting, I started a bucket list and amazingly, riding a Harley is on it. I've never ridden any kind of motorcycle in my life, but I specifically put "Harley" because it's so iconic. Getting the chance to complete one of my bucket list items so quickly has me agreeing to meet him for coffee without even screening him over the phone first. I suggest a place in downtown Windset that opened a few months ago, with topnotch coffee, delightfully sinful pastries, and avocado toast.

Looking exactly like his photos down to the easy-care blue button shirt, Bob is in line to place his order when I arrive. He recognizes me too, sticking out his hand with a stiff arm that keeps me at a respectable distance while we shake. His lips don't form much of a smile, or maybe his mustache keeps me from seeing it. You know how in romance novels the couples sometimes feel an instant chemistry? Well it's the opposite with Bob, who triggers an instant anti-chemistry, which is probably for the best because now I know to concentrate all my focus on convincing him to take me for a spin on the Harley with no expectation of favors in return.

I make small talk about weather and traffic as we wait to place our orders. He chooses an iced coffee and a mini-cupcake, I get an avocado toast and double latte. As a demonstration of my good will, I offer to treat and he accepts without argument. After we're seated, I ask if he's been a postmaster for long.

"Twenty-seven years."

"You must like the job."

"It's okay."

"Any anecdotes? Bizarre things people tried to ship, or anything like that?"

"I can't discuss official postal business." He throws a furtive glance over his shoulder, like government spies might be lurking behind him.

"That sounds very cloak and dagger. Do you have security clearance?"

"Like I said, I can't talk about it."

"Okay, sure." I give him a few minutes silence as an opportunity for him to broach a different subject, but when he doesn't take it, I feel obliged to toss another topic into the ring. "Are you considering retirement?"

He frowns and shifts in his chair. "Not really."

"I mean, do you have some hobbies you'd like to pursue?"

"Maybe."

I give him time to expand on this, but nope. "In your profile, you said you love going to museums. Are there any particular ones you're hoping to visit someday?"

"I would have to research that."

"How about hiking? Where would you want to go?"

"I'm not sure."

I feel the urge to punch him in the stomach to make the words come out. Luckily there's a table between us.

"The thing is," he says. "I always pictured retiring with my wife."

Oh man.

"Phyllis was the planner. We liked doing most of the same things. I always left it up to her."

"I'm sorry for your loss."

"It's been five years. I still can hardly say the word... *retirement*... 'cause we were gonna do it together."

"You must have something you enjoy doing."

"My bike. I love my Harley."

"You don't miss Phyllis when you're riding?"

He shakes his head. "She hated it."

I feel for Bob. I really do. But he kind of needs to move on from Phyllis for online dating to ever work for him. I take a bite out of my avocado toast and stare out the window. Bob seems content with the quiet.

This is when I see the silver Mercedes sedan with the dent on the right bumper and Red Sox decal on the left rear window, the car belonging to the mysterious guy who came to Mom's viewing. It's paused at a stoplight in front of the coffeeshop.

I spring to my feet. "That guy. I have to talk to him. It's about my dead mother." The light turns green. "Shit, he's leaving." An idea leaps into my head. "Your motorcycle. Can we ride it? It's essential I catch up to him. I've been trying to find him, but I don't even know his name."

To my surprise, Bob stands right up. "Follow me."

When we rush out the front door with me describing the car we're about to chase, Bob leads me to his Harley where we throw on helmets—he has a spare—and a minute later we're on the road, following Red Sox guy.

Bob has such a dull, low-key personality, I'm not expecting much out of this chase and I'm only loosely holding the handles when suddenly he stamps on the accelerator and zooms through a light that has just turned red. Literally there's a car starting through the intersection that has to slam on its brakes, stopping inches from us, and I nearly fly off the back when I lose my grip on one side. This might be a little too much excitement for me, but then heavy traffic forces Bob to slow down.

"Can you see the Mercedes?" I shout.

"Not yet..." He scoots over double yellow lines to pass the car in front of us, not a legal move as far as I know.

"Wait, I see it. Red Sox decal, right?" he says.

"Yeah!"

"It's getting on the highway." Bob swerves into the left lane just ahead of a pickup truck that has to hit the brakes to avoid clipping us. He maneuvers around other cars to reach the highway before them, revealing an aggressive, risk-taking side to his character in contrast to what was on display at the restaurant.

The highway is crowded but it doesn't stop Bob speeding along the shoulder till we are able to merge in, while I hang on for dear life and close my eyes, muttering to myself. Mid-prayer, I notice a growing sensation between my legs caused by the vibration of the seat. *Woah, baby.* Has my focus been all wrong? Who needs a man when you've got this?

A minute later Bob hammers the brakes, abruptly ending my brief journey toward orgasm when I slam into his back. Traffic has come to a stop, maybe due to an accident up ahead, and perhaps several that Bob caused behind us.

"Can you see anything?" I call out.

A minute later he shouts, "There it is!" With renewed excitement, he shifts in between lanes and accelerates. I pray no one from any of the stopped cars chooses to open their door to check out the highway parking lot, or we'll be dead.

"Coming up on our right," Bob yells.

I peer over his shoulder at a black BMW sedan with a Red Sox decal showing a baseball, not a pair of socks, on the top right back windshield. "That's not it!" I yell back, but I guess he doesn't hear me, because he rolls right up to the driver's side window and knocks on it.

A young woman with bright red hair is texting. She looks up at the knock and to my surprise, lowers the window a bit. "What is it?"

"My friend needs to let you know your mother died," Bob says, getting the story all wrong.

She looks at me in horror. "What?!"

"No, it's my mother who died. Sorry! Wrong car!"

She makes a face and raises her window.

Bob looks back at me. "The Red Sox are a popular team around here," he says.

If you need the obvious stated, Bob is your man.

"Let's get back!" I shout. "Take your time, though!" I readjust myself on the seat.

Bob ignores the last instruction, because our trip back to my car closely matches our prior pursuit of the Mercedes owner.

"Thanks." I stagger off the Harley, deciding a new vibrator might be better company than Bob and his motorcycle, and will require less maintenance.

"I had a nice time," Bob says. "Can I see you again?"

17

MR. PERFECT

I put a checkmark next to *Ride a Harley* on my bucket list and a cross-out line through *Bob* on my dating list. I would've liked him better if the fun-loving, adventurous side of him came out more in his conversation, and the risk-averse side governed his motorcycle riding.

Since Michael still has not replied, I try to push him out of my mind. I've sadly neglected my digital design class since Mom's passing in favor of working on my new painting. It's developed in surprising ways and I may nearly be done with it, though I don't feel quite ready to show it to Jackie. I know I'm being terribly impractical, because if someday I choose to leave Anthony, I'm going to need an independent source of income. On the other hand, I've spent years being the responsible one, and for now I'm reveling in the freedom of doing whatever I damn well please.

After a few hours painting, I drive to Longfoot Beach and experience a flash of PTSD reliving my traumatic submersion in the one-degree-colder-and-it-would-be-ice-water. Then when I picture the moon lighting Michael's face, I feel a dull sensation in my chest at the realization I'll probably never have a chance to get to know this man.

Putting all that behind me, I square my shoulders and set out across the sand while the lowering sun streaks the sky with yellows and purples. The long trek to the far end of the beach brings to mind Lawrence of Arabia, only with extreme cold instead of heat. Lawrence of Antarctica, perhaps. The wind blows bitter from the north, but that's what long johns, down jackets, and scarves are for. By the time I return to my car, my entire body quivers with life and goosebumps, and a sense of confidence fills me along with the conviction that if I check right now, I'll find a response from Michael.

And sure enough, here it is. *Oh my god.* I blow out air and rub my frozen palms on my pants. What if he says *get lost*? I stare across the parking lot at whitecaps pirouetting across the gray sea. I'm being silly, it's not a big deal, so what if the man doesn't like me? Nothing's going to come of this experiment anyway. He can't possibly be very interested in me, after taking this long to reply. Armed with feigned indifference, I look down at my phone and read his message.

I'm sorry to be so late replying to your message. I haven't checked in quite a while because I've been overwhelmed having to pack up / sell / give away / burn in effigy all the relics of the life I've lived for the last twenty (very) odd years. In other words, my ex and I sold the house and I let the deadline for moving creep up on me so that I had six months' worth of work to do in two weeks. 😱

But now it's done, thank god. I hope you were able to enjoy the beautiful sunshine today. I was happy going for a walk in a park near where I live. Afterward I had the pleasure of reading your message and finding out you liked my profile. I like yours too. 😊 *I wonder if you might want to talk on the phone sometime? My fingers are still stiff from typing my profile, including the many rough drafts of it I had to trash.*

He left his phone number at the end of the message.

A gleeful sound squeaks out of me. I love how he doesn't really comment on my profile or my photos. I would hate if he said *I love your smile* or *you look young* or (eek!) *you're so sexy.* Anything like that would strike me as phony, or something only a bot would say. I love that he isn't forcing anything. He has a reasonable excuse for his late reply, and doesn't trash his ex-wife or jump into asking me about my own (presumably) failed marriage. Just commenting on how beautiful the day was, and how nice it would be to talk sometime.

He left his phone number following his full name, Michael Duskin. *He left his full name.* I turn on the car to blow some heat at myself and dive into an Internet search. A stroke of luck occurs when I discover he's the only Michael Duskin in Massachusetts. He lives in Fairview, along Buzzard's Bay, about an hour's drive from here, not that I'm planning to ever go there, but it's good to know.

For better or worse, he doesn't have a large presence online. I see him and his ex-wife listed as co-owners of a home, and though that must've changed, I can't verify where he's currently living. There's not much else aside from a link to his business website, which looks professional if not exciting. I could turn it into something that would wow his potential clients if he let me. He has excellent reviews on Yelp—quality construction, great communication, really nice guy, etc. The only bad review said the person called, left a message, and never heard back. Some people are assholes on Yelp. Trashing someone's business with a one star when they may have just accidentally overlooked your only message is a dick move.

I find an article about him building something for free for a local charity. *C'mon.* Next I'll be reading he crossed the North River by walking on water. *Nobody could be this perfect,* I tell myself, wondering if he's a con artist using Michael Duskin's identity. I'll need to get him on FaceTime to confirm the man behind the profile looks the same as the pictures on the app, the photo on his website, and the man I saw at the beach. But what if it's true he has no flaws? If so, I hope the *opposites attract* principle applies here, because I've got a crapload of them. I've already lied about being divorced, which is a really shitty thing to do.

He's right, we need to get on the phone, even if we don't do video right away; messaging isn't going to give us the full picture. When you're talking to someone, so much is conveyed by tone of voice, hesitations, omissions, excitement level—it's a world of meaning beyond what can be written. And if I hesitate to respond, it leaves an opening for perhaps dozens of hopefuls who could be composing their winning messages to Mr. Perfect here at this very moment. I could be seconds away from being ghosted if I don't call him now.

I've spent too much of my life running in place, not taking risks, settling for a boring existence. I call his number and my heart races while the phone rings once, twice, three times.

Then he answers.

18

BEEF WELLINGTON

"**H**i is this Michael?" I greet him breathlessly.

"Vicki?" he says.

"Yes." Of course it's *Vicki*, even if it was on the tip of my tongue to say *Viola*. "I got your message."

"Hey, thanks for calling," he says.

I like his voice immediately. It's deep and warm and sounds like what I remember coming out of the guy at the beach.

"You live in Windset?" he asks.

"Right." The lie slips out easily. I suppose I could get used to this double life.

"I have a friend who lives there. Tony Vreeman. We kind of lost touch."

"I don't know him." Possibly because my mother was the Windset resident, not me.

"I guess it would've been surprising if you did. It's funny how we do that. I live in Fairview but sometimes when I meet people, they ask if I know Joe Somebody in Boston. Weirdly, one time I actually did."

"I believe we're all deeply connected to one another in New England. Might be the inbreeding, I don't know."

"Have a relative on the Mayflower?"

"Dozens. How about you?" Though there's been a welcome influx of immigrants in recent years, we still have two main factions in Massachusetts. Those who claim Mayflower ancestry like I do on my dad's side—an absurd amount of people, considering the boat held little more than a hundred passengers and crew—and the Irish.

"I'm Irish," Michael says. Folks in Massachusetts still call themselves Irish even if their family arrived in 1850 during the potato famine.

"Did your ancestors come during the potato famine?"

"How'd you know?"

When a car honks on the street closest to me, he asks if I'm driving.

"Still in the parking lot. I just finished my grocery shopping." I don't mention the beach in case it reminds him of when he tried to save me.

"What are you having for dinner?" he says.

"Um, lobster bisque, Beef Wellington with a side of truffles, and baked Alaska."

"Are you descended from Julia Child?"

"Oh wait, that was the meal I was picturing in my head. I'm really having spaghetti with marinara sauce that comes in a jar. How about you?"

"I'm having whatever I can find in the freezer."

"Good luck."

"I'll need it," he says. "How would you feel about meeting in person in a couple days?"

I catch my breath, thinking no, I shouldn't be doing this, but *yes, yes, yes,* I want to. "That sounds nice," I say after a hesitation.

"You don't seem sure."

"I am. I want to. I'm just a little nervous. I haven't done this in a while."

"Had a date, you mean?"

"Right. It's been a long time."

"Have you dated since your divorce?"

Not since my marriage if you don't count whatever that was with Bob. But now I'm worried Michael will think something's wrong with me and that's why no one is interested. "I haven't been online for long," I say.

"Me neither. If it makes you feel better, we don't have to call it a date. Just two people meeting up to see if they could be friends."

"Or to see if they could be lovers?" This represents the remains of *fuck it* night leaping out of my mouth. I don't have time to play at being friends. I need to keep the focus on my goal—a wondrous night of sexual connection shared with a man who isn't my husband, to balance the wrong Anthony did me, when he and my mother built the fake foundation to our now foundering marriage.

A nerve-wracking silence follows during which I'm sure Michael is finished with me. Then, "You're very direct, aren't you?"

"In some ways." Not so direct as to admit I lied about being divorced, though.

"I like that," he says. We agree on where to meet before signing off.

Ghostly Mom appears on the car's passenger seat. *Lovers??*

"Don't start with me,"

19

———

THE MAKEOVER

Two days later I nearly freak out when I wake up and look in the mirror. My eyes are puffy, my dyed hair shows an inch of gray roots, and I could swear three brand new wrinkle lines have suddenly sprouted on each side of my face.

What was I thinking when I agreed to a date with Michael? Obviously I had forgotten what I look like. These days, it happens a lot. I'm walking along, minding my own business, my thoughts deep in the past before I was an old person, and then, boom, I look up and see my reflection in a mirror or a window or a friggin' unexpected puddle of water, and I have no clue who that person is.

Weirdly, I barely thought about my appearance at all before zooming with Larry or going out for coffee with Bob. I remind myself Michael is just another old person too. But when I saw him at the beach, I thought he looked younger than me. Mom says men always look younger because they have thicker skin. I'll need thick skin to get through this date.

It's too late for me to book a facelift, but there ought to be time today for a hair appointment and—glancing at my chipped polish—a manicure. I spend the next hour on the phone making calls all over the region but everyone is booked.

When I call Jackie, my first word to her is, "Help!"

"Calm down, kiddo. It can't be that bad or you would've called 9-1-1."

"I need a hair appointment and a manicure today!"

"Ooh, hot date? So now you've filed for divorce?"

"This is just a casual meeting with a potential friend."

"You didn't file, in other words. By the way, you sound as casual as a house on fire. I suppose it's not for me to judge. Let me make a few calls and I'll get back to you. Hang in there."

Jackie's influence in Windset must run deep, because five minutes later I have the appointments. On my way to the stylist, I'm wondering whether I should change things up, go for a more youthful look. I've always kept my hair long—it might be time to go all Jamie Lee Curtis, or experiment with a weird color like blue or pink, but I chicken out when I reach the beautician's chair, frightened I'll be stuck with a style I hate for months. I do let her talk me into hair tinsel, though.

I'm feeling bolder by the time I arrive for my manicure and decide on nail extensions with a glittery gold polish. They're not crazy long, but afterward I wave them around watching them catch the light. What I most love about them is they would give Anthony a panic attack.

Jackie texts while I'm getting the manicure: *Meet me at Anthropologie when you're done.*

I've heard of the place but never crossed its threshold. Years have passed since I bought anything more exciting than flannel pajamas from L.L. Bean. I can see Jackie has directed me to the right place when I can't decide whether the first item I'm looking at is meant to be a shirt or pants. Obviously, this store caters to the young and hip.

Jackie has already tried something on and is waving at me from the dressing room. "Vi, over here!" she shouts.

On my way there, a store employee waylays me and offers to be my dedicated assistant, which I know means they'll have the excuse to charge me triple the going rate for everything I purchase. I figure it will all be worth it when the perfect outfit takes fifteen years off my age.

Jackie has on a sparkly purple gown. "For the art show," she says.

"I love it." I really do.

"I've got a few more to try. I see you've got help. Hi Robin."

Am I surprised Jackie knows the saleswoman? Not a bit.

"Help her find something sexy," Jackie tells her.

I spend the next two hours trying things on. I end up with sleek black pants, a tight, form-fitting deep red top with buttons I can open to show cleavage, a fitted tan leather jacket, and boots with a nice heel to them. Not too spiky or I'd be bound to fall over.

Jackie looks me over with an appraising eye. "If I was a lesbian, I'd totally date you."

I buy the ensemble and she gets the purple glitter dress. "I'm coming back to your house," she says. "You need help with your makeup."

"I don't wear makeup."

"That's what I mean."

Needless to say, when we get back to the house, I allow Jackie to make me up with some foundation, a bit of sparkly eyeshadow, and a sort of light rosy brown lipstick. "You're good at this," I say when I check myself in the mirror.

"You know what's the secret to being beautiful?" Jackie says.

I grab my cell. "Wait, let me make a note on my phone." I'm expecting the name of a miraculous beauty product.

"Confidence."

"Is that the name of the company? What's the product?"

"No, silly, I mean confidence. When you truly believe you look fabulous, others believe it too."

"Mm." It sounds like a self-help seminar, but then I look at Jackie and I see this glow she has that lights up her face and puts color in her cheeks and makes me want to be her friend always because of this positivity she has about life and love and all the things that matter. "I'll try it."

"One more thing before you go. While you were in the shower, I was looking at your new painting. Come here." She leads me over to my easel in the family room. "Lady, you have some freaky shit going on inside your head."

I have painted Mom's chair as if it's the star of a horror movie. It has claw feet, the folds at the tips of the armrests look like talons, the splotchy yellow fabric appears hairy, the background is pure darkness. A girl of seven or eight who looks much as I did at that age sits at its center, tiny compared to the chair. The indents in the cushion surrounding her appear to be jagged teeth, giving the overall effect that a villainous chair is swallowing her. The girl's pale face reflects a quiet terror that might evoke comparisons to Munch's *Scream* though my style is different.

"It's horrifying," I say. "Sorry. I'll try for something sweeter next time."

"Oh, I'm submitting this. Whether they love it or hate it, they'll stop and take notice," Jackie picks up one of my small paintbrushes. "Sign it."

"I'm not sure it's done."

"Looks done to me. I'm already pushing the rules getting the judges to consider it at this late date."

I sign it. What does it matter? The likelihood of it being picked is zilch.

"What are you calling it?" Jackie asks.

I stare at it for a minute. "Deceit."

Jackie leaves with the painting and I take a last glance at the mirror before rushing out to Mom's car, where the sensation of tiny pins sticking me all over reminds me how I felt when I was thirteen years old going out for my first official date with Reggie who had braces.

20

DR. DAD

Mom has again hitched a ride in my passenger seat, and insists on debating the merits of calling the whole thing off. She is consistent in taking Anthony's side and doing her best to talk me out of *destroying my marriage*. But her arguments have the opposite of the intended effect by reminding me I still haven't forgiven either of them and I'm determined not to let them tell me how to live my life anymore.

I'm running late and I make myself even later by slowing at every intersection and considering whether to swoop into a U-turn and head directly back home. *What the hell am I doing?* Oddly, I'm no longer even considering what might happen to my marriage, I'm imagining my dismay if I have to watch Michael's expression sink into a disappointed grimace as he gets his first glimpse of me inside a room with electric lighting as opposed to outside at night on the beach. While I'm fretting over this and acting like a freaking self-absorbed maniac, Mom nearly gets me to turn back with *you won't have a dime left for self-care once the divorce is final,* but I shout "la-la-la-la-la" until her voice grows silent.

The outside temperature has dipped into the low-twenties, and when I swerve into the Pilgrims Pub parking lot at seven minutes past four, Mom's front-wheel drive Cadillac slides on a patch of ice. I can handle it, I'm a born and bred New Englander, but as I ease back into my own lane, I nearly smush a squirrel.

Damn, that would be embarrassing if right now he's watching me kill wildlife, or if later he saw the flattened corpse sticking out from under my tire. He'd think I was an animal-hater or terrible driver, and neither one is an attractive quality in a person.

I don't park too near the restaurant so I can survey the entrance before making my approach. Popping a breath mint, I instantly spit it back out, because it's weird to be sucking on something when you meet someone for the first time.

I scan the area without seeing anyone who looks like Michael, but I'm late so he might be inside already. This is it, now or never. My hands shake as I get out of the car, beep it locked, and set out toward the bar with faltering steps. The frigid breeze burns my face, no doubt turning my nose and cheeks bright red, so I expect to look like I'm wearing clown makeup momentarily. Still, I force myself forward and I'm almost to the sidewalk when I spot him through the window glass. My heart swoons, seeing as how he looks even more fetching in full light. I watch as he notices me, recognizes me—whether from the plunge or my photos on the app, I don't know—and smiles at me. Whoa, he has a great smile, I swear his eyes are literally sparkling like he sprinkled them with fairy dust.

Pulsating with excitement, I pay no attention where I step and all at once my foot slides out from under me and up into the air. My balance lost, I crash backwards onto the concrete. One second I was upright and now I'm flat on my rear with the wind knocked out of me.

"Vicki?"

I recognize Michael's voice from the beach and our phone call, but yet again it takes a moment to recall that I'm Vicki.

He kneels down beside me. "Are you all right?"

Tears blind me but I hasten to assure him I'm okay.

"Should I call 9-1-1?"

"Oh no, there's nothing broken." As I try to pull myself up, he grasps my elbow and raises me. "Ow," slips out of me in response to the throbbing in my hip.

"Your hand is bleeding," he says.

Apparently I slammed it on the pavement trying to stop my fall. The palm is scraped and bloody, and my wrist aches.

"We really should get you checked out," he says.

"No, I'm okay, let's go in." I try to take a step but it's lucky he's holding me or I probably would've slipped again.

"Whoa. At least let me bandage that. I've got a first aid kit in my car. Will you trust me to dress the wound?"

"Are you a doctor?"

"My kids call me Dr. Dad."

"Close enough."

With him so near, I smell his shampoo or cologne, an outdoorsy scent of leather and wood mingled with something fragrant, maybe allspice. I resist pressing my nose against his neck for a better whiff.

"You can walk?"

"Judging by my performance so far, it's debatable."

"Hang onto me."

My heart beats faster as he wraps my good hand around his arm, leads me to his black Lexus SUV, and directs me to sit in the driver's seat. "I'll get the kit," he says.

Here is when I look sideways at the passenger seat and recoil in horror. Empty cans, fast food wrappers, dirty rags, an old banana peel, and stuff I can't even identify cover the seat and the floor in front of it. He comes around to that side and tosses everything into the back. I can't help but turn to see where exactly it's going, and I suppress a shudder at what looks like an actual garbage dump back there. Among other things, there's a couple of chipped end tables, a box of used paperbacks, a crate of dusty dishes, a pair of ancient oars, something that looks like an engine, and a sewing machine I swear must be from 1945.

If this is the typical state of his vehicle, he's a total slob. I, on the other hand, am a neat freak. I almost laugh out loud. It's official now, the man is human.

"Sorry for the smell. It's stuff I still haven't managed to get rid of since the move." He tosses his keys onto the center console. "You might want to lower your window."

I do. I need fresh air, despite the cold.

He gets out a cleansing pad, ointment and a bandage from the first aid kit. "Anesthesia?"

"What have you got? Weed? Crack cocaine?"

"Aspirin."

"Thanks, I'll pass."

I hope he knows I was kidding about the weed. He gets to work dressing my wound, an act that feels intimate with this person I've only just met. The tenderness of his hands touching mine distracts me from the pain of the cuts and sting of the disinfectant.

"I'm sorry I ruined our date," I say. "I mean, our potential friends meeting. Oh god, that sounds like we're Quakers."

"Potential lovers meeting." He gives me a sly smile. "Who says you ruined it? This part doesn't count. The meeting hasn't begun yet."

"I haven't scared you off by falling? You probably think I'm a klutz now."

"If it was summer, sure. But this time of year, you get a free pass due to ice."

He puts the finishing touch on his bandage. "How are you feeling?"

"Like a new woman." Actually, I'm going to have a giant bruise on my hip and leg, but I don't think it's anything serious.

We agree to return to the pub. "Ouch, I saw you fall," the hostess says when we get inside. "You gonna be okay?"

"Yeah, my new doctor fixed me up," I say.

"I had to perform the surgery without anesthesia," Michael says.

"I bit down on the seatbelt to keep from screaming."

"Sure, whatever." The hostess leads us to a high-top table.

When Michael helps me off with my jacket and pulls out my chair for me, he says, "Should we start over? Pleasure to meet you, Vicki."

"It's Viola." The truth comes out of me, though I had not planned to tell him. "I used a fake name because I was worried about scammers. My name's Viola."

"Viola. That's beautiful," he says.

I get a chance to really look at him now. My date, with gray hair neatly parted, wears a navy blue hoodie under his winter jacket, faded jeans, and Doc Martens. It's hard to resist reaching over to rub my hand through his whiskers. He probably spent five minutes preparing himself to go out, compared to my full day. It doesn't matter. I love that he looks and acts like he could move effortlessly between a Fortune 500 company boardroom and a construction job site.

"It's weird, isn't it?" he says.

"What do you mean?"

"Do you feel like you're on a job interview?"

"Sort of."

"When we were in our twenties, we met people accidentally and gradually got to know them. But meeting like this—there's pressure to make a good impression instantly. Did you bring a list of questions?"

"I thought I'd let you fill them out later online."

"I imagine you want to know my religion, politics, and ideas for peace in the Middle East?"

"Well, it would be nice if they perfectly aligned with mine. Especially my Mideast solution—I've worked it all out. But I'll be happy if you're not planning to push your views on me, whatever they are."

"I won't if you won't."

"Deal." I gaze into those sparkly brown eyes of his again and don't even notice when the waitress arrives to take our orders until she asks for a second time in a louder voice.

"Chardonnay, please," I say.

"Can I get a mojito mocktail?" Michael asks.

"Sure," she says.

"Bruschetta to share?" he asks me.

I nod, distracted by his mocktail order. When the server leaves, I say, "You don't drink?" in a squeaky voice resulting from the *danger* alarm buzzing in my head. First the filthy car, now the possibility that he's an alcoholic. *What if he only quit last month?* I knew his profile sounded too perfect.

"Sober for thirty-two years," he says.

"Wow, good for you." My relief is audible. I'd be lucky to have a fraction of his self-control, plus now I'm excited at the prospect of a designated driver. "Does it bother you if I drink?"

"I wouldn't have suggested a pub if it did."

"I guess not."

"It feels good to sit. Things have been crazy for me lately, between work and moving out of my house. I had no idea how much of a packrat I am until now."

"It's amazing how stuff accumulates."

"Right? Did you have to move too?"

I prepared in advance for this question. "I moved to my mom's house, which was helpful for both of us." It's not really a lie if I don't say when and for how long. "But she passed away last week, and now I need to sell the house."

"I'm sorry for your loss."

"Thank you." My eyes well up and I dab them with my napkin. "It was really sudden. She was still enjoying her life. After she died, I found out she was on a date when she keeled over. And she was eighty-nine!"

"Funny, I thought *I* might be too old for dating."

"Turns out we're on the low end of our age group."

"Why can't you keep your mom's house? Do you have siblings?"

Because I actually live in California with my husband, I don't say. "No, my brother's gone too. But the place needs work."

"Oh man, your brother too?"

"He passed a long time ago. Aids."

"That's awful."

"Mm. I miss him a lot. He would've made a huge difference in my life, if he'd been around. Would've helped me realize my marriage was in a shambles."

"Sorry. I might be able to help with your mother's house, though. I'm a contractor. Would you like me to look at it?"

"Wait, do you use the dating app to get new jobs?"

"How else am I supposed to find work?"

"Okay, sure, I don't blame you. Can you hire me to redesign your website?"

"What's wrong with my website?"

"Nothing, if the year is 1998."

"You're a website designer?"

"I could be. I'm studying graphic design." When I'm not painting, that is. I feel a sudden urge to pee. "Excuse me, I need to use the restroom."

"If you haven't returned in ten minutes I'll assume I didn't make the cut."

"Promise to hire me and I'll guarantee not to slip out the back."

"Fine if you'll let me write up an estimate for your house."

"Deal."

Our drinks and appetizers have arrived by the time I return. "Have you built a lot of houses?" I ask.

He nods. "Houses and townhouses. Individual and developments. Never had any complaints about any of them."

"You must be good."

"Quality's important to me."

"Have you always built homes?"

"I started out working in the car industry. But I moved on after some insane shit happened. Anyway, I like building more than selling. I trained as a carpenter before forming my own company."

He asks about my background, and I tell him about my career in tech writing. "I wanted to be an artist but I didn't want to starve," I say.

"What made you so sure you wouldn't succeed?"

I shrug. It's a question I often ask myself. "I don't know."

"I was the same way for a while. That's why I began in sales. I didn't think I could make enough doing what I enjoyed."

"But then you did. What changed?"

"My attitude."

Our time together passes quickly in easy conversation. When I finish my wine, I say no to the server asking if I'd like another. A man who doesn't drink might think a woman who downs two glasses is a lush.

When the server returns with the check, Michael reaches for his wallet.

"Please let me pay," I say.

"You'll regret it when you see my bill for medical services."

"Hmm."

He hands his credit card to the server.

"Thank you," I say.

In the parking lot, we pass his car on the way to mine. "The stuff in my car... that's just a tiny fraction of the junk I've had to deal with."

"You selling that stuff?"

"Are you buying?"

"No, I have junk to get rid of too."

"That's what everyone says. I have to beg people to take things for free."

He shakes my uninjured hand and draws me into a quick half-hug, the kind of motion you do with someone you aren't really friends with yet. "You're a lovely person," he says.

"Thank you." I probably should say something nice back, but I'm trying to parse if this means he really likes me, or if it's a polite brush-off.

"Have a safe drive home," he says.

As I start up Mom's car, a feeling of heaviness falls over me. Should I be disappointed he made no attempt to come back to my place for the night, or even to give me a sterile peck on the cheek? I suspect I will never hear from this man again—a thought that bothers me far more than it should.

21

____

THE MURAL

After resolving to tackle a few of the jobs involved in settling Mom's estate, I'm on the phone all morning, confounded by the level of complexity involved in transferring an IRA from a deceased person to the one person who is inheriting from her.

Anthony calls at noon, probably because he's having no luck reaching me in the evenings, and I'm positively chatty with him though I'm not sure why. Maybe as I grow emotionally farther from him, he seems like less of a threat. Maybe if we get divorced, we could be friends. Maybe coyotes can fly.

My hours spent staring at the family room walls while waiting on hold and speaking to my husband have given me an idea. The place cries out for a fresh coat of paint, and who better to do it than me? I did an excellent job on the interior of my California home last year and thoroughly enjoyed myself. Two more benefits are the huge savings over paying a contractor, and the excuse I'll have to further delay my return to Anthony.

After breakfast I head to the hardware store to pick out the paint colors. I'm confining myself to the family room first; one section at a time. My initial thought is to go with a neutral shade like tan or beige, but when I see all the bright colors available, I can't resist buying a variety. I'm not even sure what I'm going to do with them until, during my drive back home, I picture a mural on the family room wall, the one without windows. As soon as the idea comes to me, I get this bubbly feeling inside and I know I've got to do it, though I have no plans yet for what it will look like, other than—since it's a seaside home—it must have an ocean theme.

It feels so good to be physically active, blasting my favorite playlist of random songs I like while I work. I move the furniture toward the center of the room before taking down everything that's attached to the wall. I spread out a tarp to protect the wood floor and carpet, and stick masking tape around all the edges to preserve the trim. All this activity helps distract me from agonizing over the lack of communication from Michael, who sent only the brief message, *I had a nice time, hope there won't be a malpractice suit*, to which I replied *thanks doc, I had a nice time too and my lawyer will be in touch*, followed by a mischievous devil emoji. Then he added he would be very busy finishing up a job, but he would reach out after that. I wonder if this is his way of letting me down gradually by putting me off for a few days at a time till I become sick of waiting and turn my attention elsewhere.

By noon I have my paints ready to go, particularly the blue, green, and white I'll need for the ocean and sky. Brush in hand, I pause and glance over at Mom's chair. "Any ideas what I should paint?"

Giant portrait of your beloved mother?

I shiver at the thought of it. "This is not your memorial, Mom." I dip my brush and sweep a bold stroke of marine blue across the wall while Freddie Mercury sings *Don't Stop Me Now*. I feel light as a cloud.

"You know, I might not sell the house after all."

Anthony won't like that.

"Do you think I care what he thinks?"

Stop it, you're scaring me.

"Funny, me scaring the ghost."

You might want to check out the property tax bill before rushing into anything.

"I have to live somewhere. Why not here?"

Any idea what it costs to heat this place?

"So many unknowns. Maybe I can afford it if I do any necessary work myself. Or maybe Michael will give me a good price for remodeling the bathrooms like you wanted to do."

There might be a price for that good price.

"I can always hope."

After I've worked for an hour, my phone pings which makes my heart ping hopefully for a message from Michael. Nope, it's spam. *Dear woman-we-don't-know, we want to offer you a job that's perfectly suited to your skills we know nothing about.* I return to my depiction of the sea, which, along with a stretch of sky at the top, will be the backdrop for everything else that appears on the wall. The days pass with me immersed in the wonderful and frustrating act of creation.

Until a call I've been hoping for comes in.

22

GOOD NEWS SO FAR

"You're in, kiddo," Jackie says.

"What?"

"The Windset Art Society. They want your painting in the show."

I let out a whoop. "That's fantastic! But wait a minute. This wasn't just you strong-arming them, was it?"

"Absolutely not. My influence only got you considered after the deadline. They take judging artistic merit seriously. This is all you. They get a million submissions of boats, lighthouses, and lobsterpots. Trust me, they love when they can bring something different into the show."

"Okay. Cool. What now?"

"I can make you a gorgeous frame. I'll wave my rush fee just for you."

"You're the best."

"Stop by today and we'll go over the options. You want to sell this thing?"

"Eeek, no! It's too personal."

"Fine, no price tag. But I'll let you know if anyone makes an offer you can't refuse."

"That'll be the day."

"You need to work on your optimism. The opening night gala is next Friday. Treat yourself to a new outfit. Oh, and your painting is eligible for awards."

So much to consider, and now my phone is flashing. "My daughter's calling. I'll text you before I come by."

I pick up Max's call. In my excitement, I immediately announce that "my painting has been accepted into a juried art exhibit and I'm attending the opening gala on Friday."

"WHAT? What painting? Is this from years ago? Have I ever seen it?"

Uh oh, I should've thought this through and now I've blurted too much. "Please don't say anything to your father. I was working on the painting the last few weeks. He'll be upset that I took time for anything other than getting the estate settled."

"You deserve to take some time to heal. Grandma just died! Tell me about your painting."

"There isn't much to say. It's not that great. Of course, this is just a local show."

"Don't you dare minimize your accomplishment! Can you take a picture of it and send it to me?"

"Not right now. I don't have it here. I can do it at the show, I guess." It probably would be best if she never sees it. She might recognize that it's Grandma's chair, and me stuck in the middle of it, which could raise uncomfortable questions.

"Do you have news?" I ask. It's rare for her to call out of the blue without news.

"Yes! I've been seeing this guy, his name's Adam, he's an actor with a non-speaking role in *The Book of Mormon*, the musical I'm working on."

"I know what musical you're working on."

"Anyhow, I'm moving in with him."

"How long have you been seeing him?" And why haven't I heard about him till now?

"It's been a few months."

"That's not terribly long. What's the rush to move in with him?"

"I'm crazy about him. He's very smart, he went to NYU, and he's so talented, he'll be famous someday, you'll see."

"What's his other job?" No one can support themselves from non-speaking roles even when the musical is on Broadway.

"He works for Door Dash."

I figured.

"And I'm sick of living in a closet! He only has two roommates, and he's got a whole bedroom AND bathroom to himself."

"Well think about this carefully. What if things don't work out and you can't go back to your old place?"

"Oh Mom, you worry too much. Anyhow, I wanted to tell you that Adam is from Massachusetts too! His mother, she's divorced, she lives in Boston. I thought it might be nice for you two to meet."

I'm wondering if I really want to meet a woman whose son I may have reason to dislike if his relationship with my daughter ends unhappily. "Sure. Not right away, though. I have so much to do after having goofed off for a while." I don't mention that rather than tackling the estate, I'm now busy creating a wall mural for the house I'm supposed to be selling.

"You didn't goof off! You got some well-deserved respite and created what I'm sure must be a masterpiece. Adam is texting me, I have to hang up now. Love you so much, Mom."

"Love you so much too." It's only after she clicks off that I realize I've neglected to get Adam's last name. I text her for the information, but questions of that sort generally lie in cyberspace unanswered forever.

I stare at my phone willing Michael to call me. It's been four days since he said he would be busy but that he definitely would get in touch with me after that. Maybe he didn't say *definitely.* I want to invite him to the gala but thanks to my training as a young woman, I have great difficulty with the concept of my calling to ask a man out instead of the other way around. Particularly since I have a husband, I might add. And yet I really really want Michael to come to the gala with me.

What's the worst that can happen if I ask him? He says no because he can't make that day, but leaves things open for another time. Or he says no without mentioning any hope of another date. Or he doesn't answer or return my call and then he ghosts me.

Or he becomes furious that you've called him, finds out your address, and breaks into your house during the night to murder you, says Mom, always the dramatist.

I decide to call him just to spite her. He answers on the second ring. "How did you know I was about to call you?" he says.

"I'm a mind reader."

"What am I thinking right now?"

"That you better be careful what you think around me from now on."

"Okay, that confirms it."

"I actually called to share some good news. The painting I've been working on was accepted into a juried art exhibit."

"Congratulations! When does the exhibit start? I want to go see it."

"I'm glad you said that. There's an opening gala next Friday at this cool historic home where the exhibit is being set up. Would you be my date?"

"I'd be honored. If you text me your address and the venue location, I'll come round to pick you up."

"Thank you, sir."

When we hang up, I realize I'm shaking from the excitement. So many good things happened today. My painting was deemed worthy of an art exhibit. I have a date with a man who makes my toes tingle when I think about him. And my daughter has a new boyfriend. I hope that last one is a good thing, but I'm not quite sure.

23

———

THE MERMAID

Michael arrives a few minutes early for our date, but it's not a problem because I've been ready for an hour, pacing the house, unable to sit while I have this feeling like I've swallowed a bowl of thorns and they're poking me all over inside. Twice I tripped on the carpet thanks to my new ankle-length dress and high heels that Jackie insisted I buy, lending hope I may now be fully trained in wearing them and will have no further mishaps. I can't remember ever owning an outfit as eye-catching as this one before, with a red satin dress that's low-cut and form-hugging in a way that emphasizes the few remaining good parts thank god, paired with classic glossy black pumps. When I welcome Michael into the house, his face lights up and his admiring gaze wanders from my face down to my toes and back up again. He actually says, "Wow."

"*Wow* back at you." He has on an authentic black tux that looks new and not like something he wore twenty or thirty years ago at his wedding. This is paired with impeccable shiny black shoes and a tie featuring blue irises from a Van Gogh painting. "Love the tie," I say, imagining myself grabbing it and pulling him into a deep, sexy kiss. Unfortunately he's holding a cardboard box that blocks me from indulging my baser instincts.

"It's not too on-the-nose?"

"You mean wearing art to an art exhibit? No, it's perfect, I wish I had thought of it."

"You're a work of art yourself," he says.

"How did you know I love compliments? What would you like, my first-born child? You can have her. She's an adult now, but still high maintenance."

"Very generous of you. But I already have two high maintenance adult children." He lays down the box, allowing us to indulge in a schizophrenic hug that can't decide whether we're polite acquaintances or lovers reunited after an absence of many years.

"Is that for me?" I do a little bounce pointing at the box.

"Do you like it?"

"I love it! How'd you know I needed a box?"

"Oh, but there's something in it."

"Didn't know it was my birthday." With excitement bubbling up—because I do love receiving gifts—I plunge my hands into the package and pull out a mermaid. A copper weathervane of a mermaid, to be exact. "This is beautiful!"

"I glad you like it. I thought you might need one."

"I do. Doesn't everyone? But this is too much. You only just met me." *I may already be having hot dreams about you, but it's way too soon for gifts.*

"I didn't buy it. I took it off my roof before putting the house up for sale."

"But then you must bring it to your new house."

"I'm renting an apartment."

"If you buy later, I mean."

"I want you to have it. You have the perfect seaside home for it." He inserts a pregnant pause before throwing the conversation in a surprising direction. "You know, I thought you might be a mermaid the first time I met you." His eyes glisten with amusement.

If I were a teenager, I'd be blushing right now. "When did you figure out it was me?" I ask.

"As soon as I saw your pictures on the app."

"I admit I was hoping you wouldn't make the connection. I was so shitfaced, and I'm normally not much of a drinker." Another memory pops into my head. "Oh god, when I slipped in the parking lot on our first date... I hope you didn't think I'd been drinking again."

"I wouldn't blame you. There's a lot of pressure when you're meeting a stranger the first time, praying they don't turn out to be a raving lunatic."

"I'm glad we can talk about this now. I felt terrible about not thanking you."

"Is that why you looked me up on the app?"

"Huh? No. I didn't do that. I never imagined you might also be on the dating app. It was the software that found you out there in the sea of possible matches, and put you on my list."

He tilts his head toward me. "Do you believe in fate?"

"I'm not sure. It feels powerful when something like this happens."

"There's something about you that feels familiar... I felt it at the beach too. It bothered me I didn't know how to find you afterwards. And then when I saw you on the app, it seemed like we were supposed to meet."

I'm moved by this, but considering my current matrimonial state, it doesn't seem the right time to agree to the sentiment. "It was very kind of you to come to my rescue," I say instead.

"Even though you didn't need rescue?"

"All that counts is I looked like I needed it." I check the time. "I wanted to show you the house, but I'm afraid we have to get going."

He gallantly gets the door for me, but as soon as I see the stairs, I look down at my high heels and remember how I've already fallen twice in them. I duck back inside, put on my winter boots, and carry my dress shoes to change into at the event. On our way down to the street, I remember the junk heap inside Michael's car and wonder if I will end up with the sticky residue of spilled soda stuck to the backside of my gown. But when he opens the passenger side, I gape into a vehicle emptied of its former contents, with windows washed, panel wiped, upholstery scrubbed, and floors vacuumed.

"Wow," I say. "You clean up good."

24

DA SEAT

The parking surrounding Thornwood House is nearly full.

"A lot of folks are going to see your art," Michael says.

"That's what I'm afraid of."

"I bet they're going to love it."

A woman named Joyce checks us in, and when I tell her I'm one of the artists, she asks which piece I did. "It's a painting called *Deceit*," I say.

"The chair?" Her eyes bug out. "You did the chair?"

"Uh, yeah."

"You look so normal."

Michael widens his eyes and pinches his lips shut.

"Uh, thanks?" I say to Joyce. "Can you tell me where it is?"

We follow her directions to the "salon," where it would be impossible to miss my painting in the corner by the grand piano. Its frame, brilliantly designed by Jackie, consists of four weathered, splintered slabs of wood haphazardly assembled— as if by a serial killer in a hurry—into a crooked rectangle with rusty nails partly protruding. It snatches the viewer's gaze and flings it helplessly into the center of the demonic chair. As I watch Michael trying to wrap his head around the entire twisted presentation, it seems inevitable he will reach the conclusion that *I* am the raving lunatic he warned against.

"Go ahead. Save yourself while you still can." I fully expect him to run screaming from the room.

"This must be the coolest art I've ever seen," he says with something like awe in his tone.

"Really?" It's official. We're both certifiably cuckoo.

"I don't tell many people this, but I love horror. Books and films. And now art. This is amazing, in a terrifying sort of way."

I follow his shifting gaze to the title card and read what's printed. "*Da Seat*? I told Jackie it was *Deceit.* D-e-c-e-i-t. But this is good. That's what the painting is missing, a sense of humor."

"Where did the idea come from?" Michael says.

I was afraid he'd ask this. If he comes to the house again, which might be doubtful at this point, he'll want the tour and then he'll see the chair so there's no point in lying. "It's my mother's chair."

"Uh huh."

"Her death brought back some unresolved issues," I say lightly, like they were no worse than discovering a patch of poison ivy in the rose garden.

"Uh huh."

"But as you can see, it's obviously a work of fiction. If you look—"

"Mom!"

My mouth freezes open in mid-sentence at what sounds exactly like the voice of my daughter though of course it couldn't possibly be her.

"Mom, it's me," she says, making me turn around and confront the reality of her presence here. I still half-believe she's a ghostly visage until her solid substance smashes into my embrace. *How will I explain Michael to her?* She will tell

Anthony; she never can keep her mouth shut. Vengeance will rain down on me.

"You nearly gave me a heart attack." I stall, straining my poor brain for a solution.

"Aren't you glad I came? I couldn't miss your exhibit. Adam wanted to come but he had to work. I took the train and asked Cadence to pick me up at the station so I could surprise you. What is this?!"

I think she's referring to the painting, until she says, "YOU WON TWO BLUE RIBBONS!"

I had noticed them but hadn't had a chance to read what they were for in the confusion of explaining my art to Michael.

"Juror's Choice and Best Acrylic Painting! You're going to be famous, Mom!"

The woman standing behind my daughter steps forward with hand extended. "Congratulations. I'm Cadence Turell."

"Cadence?" I say.

Max whirls around and opens up space for her. "This is Adam's mother. Remember I said she lives in Boston?"

"Max is a doll," Cadence says.

We shake hands while she stares past me at Michael, eyeing him like she's a hawk contemplating a plump rabbit. I would like to be able to sic *Da Seat* on her, but instead I say, "This is my friend Michael Duskin from high school. We just ran into each other here." I throw him a look, pleading for him to trust me and go along with the ruse.

He tightens his brow but doesn't contradict me. Yet.

"How cool is that?" Max throws her arms around him. "I'm her daughter Max. What was she like as a teenager?"

"Trouble," he says, not missing a beat. "Nothing but trouble."

"I knew it!" Max says, beaming.

Cadence sweeps forward and takes Michael's hand. "Cadence Turell. Don't tell me you came here all by yourself?"

He flicks a glance my way. "All right, I won't."

Only now do I notice how perfectly turned out Cadence is. Her blond hair looks natural, her figure youthful, her clothing stylish, her teeth flawless, and her French manicure elegant. She is not wearing a wedding ring and her skin is remarkably smooth for someone with a kid around the same age as mine. Why is she still holding Michael's hand?

"Do you live in the area?" she asks him.

He tells her where he lives.

"What brought you to the gala tonight?"

I brought him here, I want to say, but Max is still listening.

He casts a meaningful look in my direction like he's asking for permission to tell the truth. I make it clear the answer is *no* by answering for him. "Michael likes supporting local artists."

Meanwhile my daughter is staring at my painting with her mouth hanging open in astonishment.

"Oh my god, look at this! Isn't that Grandma's chair? And that girl, she looks like me. This is incredible. You took something that's normally warm and comforting, and turned it into a nightmare vision."

"Think of it as a Grimm's Fairy Tale type of thing," I say.

"It's brilliant, Mom."

I should've guessed she'd love the drama of it.

Meanwhile Cadence has slipped her hand through Michael's arm and is drawing him away from our little group. "Have you seen the painting of the young woman on the beach? Reminds me of Andrew Wyatt."

I'm reaching for his other arm to yank him back when a man behind me says, "Excuse me, are you the artist?" I would've ignored him, except my daughter seizes my hand like a vice and says, "Mom, wait. This gentleman would like to speak to you," forcing me to turn around.

I paste a fake smile on my face. "Hi, yes, I'm Viola."

The man pumps my hand. "Delighted. I'm Tucker

Hanwell," he says in a British accent. "I own The Hanwell Gallery. Your work is fascinating."

"Mine?" I nod toward it to make sure he's not mistaking me for the creator of a far more accomplished piece. Meanwhile Cadence has disappeared with Michael and Max is on her phone, wandering off to find a quiet corner I suppose.

"*Da Seat*, no? Tell me about it. What inspired you?"

Distracted by that woman running off with my date, I've no desire to get into my mommy issues. I blurt the first answer that pops into my head. "Getting my tooth pulled."

"Ah." Tucker nods his head while staring at the chair. "Oh yes, I can see that. The little girl watches the dentist approaching. She wants desperately to run away, but the evil chair has gotten hold of her. To the girl, it seems like the seat is the monster."

I'm impressed by his imagination. "Exactly," I say.

"It's so relatable." His voice grows louder in his excitement. "It's like the feeling when you're stuck for hours in a waiting room. Say, the registry of motor vehicles. You're going out of your mind waiting for your number to be called, but you can't leave your seat because you've already invested so much of your time."

"We've all been there, done that," I put in helpfully.

"Oh. Oh. I've had another thought."

"Do tell."

"The time I flew to Thailand. I thought the plane would never land. And there was so much turbulence, we weren't allowed to get up for most of that flight from hell. Same feeling that you've shown here, like your viciously uncomfortable seat is swallowing you and you'll never get out of it. Have you thought about doing a series of these?"

"You mean, more chairs?"

"Yes, but each one holds a clue about what the situation is, whether a dentist's chair, a waiting room, a plane, a torture chamber, or whatever. A series could help put your name on the map."

"I suppose it's a possibility." I'm distracted, glancing around the salon without catching sight of Michael or Max. What if they're talking in the next room and she's telling him that her father is still very much my husband? "Could you excuse me?" I say.

He hands me his card. "Please get in touch. Maybe we could meet for drinks some time? I'd love to talk more about your work and whether it might be a fit for our gallery."

Am I detecting a bit of flirtation? If I end up divorced and Michael loses interest, I could do a lot worse. Tucker doesn't look a day older than forty-five, sporting a youthful look in a dress jacket that matches his blue eyes, paired with jeans and high tops. Why would he be interested in me, a woman who must be his senior by fifteen or more years? I do take his card, of course.

Michael's laugh echoes from the formal dining room, where food related artwork is being displayed. He and Cadence stand before a still life of the most phallic eggplant I've ever seen. Unbelievably, she still has her hand draped through his arm. I'm as indignant as I would be if she actually knew he had come here as my date. But just as I aim my steps in their direction, I hear Max calling out my name from behind.

She catches up to me. "Aren't they cute?" She nods toward Michael and Cadence. "I'm so happy for them." Spoken like they just announced their engagement. "She told me she's been really lonely since her divorce."

"Well she's too late," I say without thinking it through.

"Too late?"

"Yes. I, um, Michael is dating my friend Jackie and it's going really well."

"Oh, is she here?"

As I shift my gaze around the room, I pray she isn't with Ken.

"Viola!" she calls out from the doorway. "There you are."

She's with Ken. They hurry toward us. "Did you see your ribbons?" she says.

"I'm so grateful," I say. "Jackie, Ken, this is my daughter Max."

"So nice to meet you! You're the other high school friend, right?" Max says to Jackie.

"Other?" Jackie says.

"Great to see you, Ken!" I wedge myself between Jackie and Ken to give him a hug.

Michael is now headed our way, along with his clingy new girlfriend.

I lean into Jackie and whisper, "Follow my lead."

"Michael, look, Jackie's here," I say.

"Hey," he says, unsure what is expected from him.

Max gives me a he-seems-notably-disinterested look.

"Good to see you." Jackie thinks she's playing along when she shakes his hand.

Max suppresses a laugh.

"Can I talk to you, Viola?" Michael says.

"Sure." Everyone looks at him like they're expecting an explanation.

"We have unresolved teen trauma to discuss," he says.

Max is distracted reading something on her phone again.

"I'll be here, Michael," Cadence calls after him.

He pulls me down the hallway. "Can you explain what's going on?"

"I'm so sorry. I couldn't tell my daughter we're dating. She's been devastated by the divorce and still hopes her father and I will get back together." I know I should tell him the truth, but I'm afraid he'll walk right out, possibly straight into Cadence's arms, without giving me a chance to explain.

"She'll have to find out eventually," Michael says.

I warm to the implication that our dating will continue. "I know, I know. I'm a coward. It's just... I want to give her a little time. She'll get used to our being apart, and then I can come clean about the dating. Do you mind?"

He breathes out heavily. "Sure. I get it."

Max speed walks up behind us. "Mom, I'm so sorry, but I have to go now."

"Already?"

"I have to catch the train back tonight. I've got stuff to do in the morning."

"Let me drive you." At the same time, I remember I don't have the car with me. Michael drove us to the show.

"No, no, you need to stay here and make an impression. I've got an Uber coming." She hugs me tight. "Can I get a refund for the Uber?"

I knew that was coming.

"Nice to meet you, Michael." Max lowers her voice. "Cadence really likes you."

He smiles. "Great to meet you too, Max."

The second Max goes away, Cadence flutters toward Michael. "There's this amazing photograph in the study—"

"I promised Viola I'd help her monitor her painting. You know, get names of gallery owners and museum reps who stop by," he says. "It was very nice to meet you." He grasps her hand to shake it, intercepting her incoming embrace.

When her expression sinks, I suddenly feel sorry for her. The unfulfilled desire to be loved can make anyone screwy.

25

SIGNAL

Hard to believe no one stopped by from the Met. Still, some enthusiastic art lovers encouraged me not to give up on this mad idea of passing myself off as an artist.

I discovered that whether or not Michael and I end up getting intimate, I need to hire him as my marketing director. He told anyone within spitting distance how I am a highly regarded, award-winning artist whose work is coveted by collectors around the world. "She's on the brink of becoming a household name," he said.

He was disappointed I had neglected to print up business cards showing my profession as "International Award-winning Artist," but he made up for it by writing the words out neatly on a piece of paper with my contact information beneath, and directing everyone to take a picture of it. The information included the name of my new website, violasagewood.com, which has yet to be created. I do have a website called violabluff.com, but I'm not about to bring up my married name.

The closest Anthony ever came to promoting my skills was

when he told our neighbors I had painted the interior of our house and I could do theirs too, for the right price.

"I'm very grateful for all your help," I tell Michael after we get in his car.

"I had a blast. Hope I didn't overdo it. It just seems like someone with your talent should be encouraged to create more art."

Not knowing how to handle compliments, I change the subject. "Look at that moon." It looks like half of a liquid orange sphere resting on the ocean. "How do you feel about taking a detour?"

Michael glances sideways out my window. "Where should we go?"

"The lighthouse," I say on impulse.

"You have a boat to get there?"

"Not Farer's Light." That one marks a rocky ledge a mile offshore. "Windset Lighthouse. It's drivable. I'll direct you."

"Great, I've never been there."

"Mm. I think you'll enjoy it." We are lovers of lighthouses in New England, even those of us who have never spent a night at sea. "It's right at the breakwater with views of the harbor on one side, open ocean on the other. I don't think it has a nautical purpose anymore, but it still flashes. And of course, it's the symbolic heart of our town."

"Of course."

Ten minutes later we pull into the empty lot and Michael parks by the keeper's cottage at the base of the beautiful white lighthouse, recently restored. The windows of the cottage are dark.

"Should we knock and ask for a tour?" Michael says.

"I'm sure the keeper would be delighted to be woken from a sound sleep to open up the lighthouse for us."

"They would if they knew you're an acclaimed artist."

I bite my tongue to keep from asking, *where have you been all my life?* Then I change into my boots before stepping out of the car, where the low tide scent of seaweed and barnacles fills my nostrils and makes me grateful to be home. The air is still and the sky a silky backdrop to the glorious moon hovering above a calm sea. It casts a yellow glow over the flat rocks that form the breakwater, drawing my eye, tempting me to walk across them to the channel as I haven't done in years. "Let's go out to the end."

A moment after we start on the rough path across the rocks, Michael, seeing me wobble on an uneven spot, takes my hand. *Yikes!* His touch gives me a hot flash, something I would've thought only my more intimate parts might trigger. Actually, holding his hand feels like an enormously intimate act, though I'm pretty sure that didn't even count as one of the bases when I was a teenager. I make sure not to give him any excuse to let go while I trace the familiar trail along the breakwater.

"We can sit here," I say when we come to the end, choosing the same raised rock that forms a bench where I always sat in the past. Tragically, our hands separate with the need to warm them up in our respective pockets.

For several minutes we absorb the quiet, gazing out at moon and sea and the silhouette of shoreline. Somehow—okay, sure, it was thanks to my slowly inching toward him—we end up leaning against each other, arms pressed together, which is nearly as sexy as holding his hand.

Movement back near the lighthouse draws my eye. "Is that a German Shepherd?"

Michael follows my gaze. "Coyote."

While we watch, it sits in a spot that blocks our way off the breakwater.

"How are we going to get back?"

"We can swim. Aren't you a fan of polar plunges?"

"Ha." I bump him with my shoulder. "Think he's male?"

"Either that or a large female."

"See how he avoids our direct gaze," I say.

"He's feigning nonchalance. He looks sideways at us now and then."

"Like a man checking out an attractive woman, no?"

Michael gives me a side eye. "Don't know what you're talkin' about."

"I'm having a staring contest with him now."

"My money's on him."

"You saying I'm easily distracted?"

"Oh my god, is that a whale over there?" he says.

I whip my head around toward the sea. "Where?"

He's laughing.

"Dammit, that wasn't fair." I get out my phone. "I'm going to find out more about our new friend."

"Okay."

"Did you know January is the beginning of their mating season? Seems a bit cold to be thinking about love."

"Body heat, Viola. That's what it's all about," he says.

To my delight, he scooches closer. *C'mon baby light my fire.*

"They're more aggressive at this time. We should be careful," I say. "Do you think it's funny there's a *season* for mating?"

"I'm sure it's hard work. They need a break from it."

"I can hear people now. 'Honey, can we have sex tonight?' 'Are you kidding me? It's not the season,'" I say. "I wonder if they stop altogether when they're past child-bearing age."

"How would they know?"

"Might just lose the urge. How do you think he picks his mate? Will he search far and wide for the most beautiful or the sexiest of his kind?"

"Is that all you care about? Looks?"

"Am I shallow?"

"I don't know. What about personality?"

"That's a good point. Personalities need to match or else

they'll drive each other nuts. Do you think opposites attract though?"

"Are we opposites?" he says.

"You have whiskers, I don't. I have breasts, you don't."

"You can paint perfectly rendered chairs and people. I can't even draw a stick figure."

"You can build a house and I can barely change a light bulb." I'm not sure if this is too much information.

"We could not be more opposite," he says. "And since we like each other, opposites must attract. Theory proven."

"That was easy," I say. "Why do scientists make it sound so hard?"

"To make themselves seem useful."

The coyote stands and turns toward the parking lot. I glimpse a smaller coyote on the far side of it. "Look."

"She might be the one," Michael whispers like they can understand us.

"Is it fate or is she literally the first eligible candidate to cross his path?" The latter happened to Anthony and me.

"Oh I believe in fate."

"Do you think it's fate you and I met?"

"Without a doubt."

"It wasn't an accident you saw me on the beach that night and decided you needed to rescue me?"

"No."

We watch the male coyote trot after the female.

He nods toward the pair. "That wasn't an accident either."

The romantic in me wants to believe this. The romantic in me is searching for a deep sense of connection, a feeling that a certain man and I were meant for each other from the beginning, a sign from the heavens or the lighthouse or this thoughtful coyote that I am destined to love him, and he, me, till the end of eternity.

"Signal, I hope your lives are blessed with happiness and many healthy pups," I say.

"Amen. Signal?"

"We made a connection tonight. He should have a name."

The shaft of moonlight across the breakwater guides us back to the car.

LATER WHEN MICHAEL pulls over in front of Mom's house, I say, "Sorry you had to deal with that woman hanging all over you."

"What an ordeal." His eyes are amused. "Did you know she's Warren Buffet's daughter?"

"She... what?"

"That's right. Warren Buffet's daughter."

"You can't be serious."

"Did you see her bracelet? Real diamonds."

I didn't notice, but her sleeve might've covered it. "She must be worth billions."

"Yup. And she gave me her phone number."

My spirits plummet. Is Michael nothing more than a gold-digger? I'm curious enough to search on Buffet's children on my phone. "Are you planning to call her?"

"Wouldn't you?"

"His daughter's name is Susan," I read on Wikipedia.

"She uses an alias. Otherwise everyone would always be hitting her up for a donation."

"Susan is seventy-two. Cadence doesn't resemble her Wikipedia photo at all."

"Imagine having the money to hire the best plastic surgeon in the world. Not that *you* would need it," Michael says.

I punch him in the arm. "Liar! Your story is complete bullshit."

He laughs and grabs my wrists, keeping me from hitting him again. "Look who's talking," he says.

"At least I had a good reason for it. I wanted to protect my daughter's feelings." For a second or two, I almost buy my own bullshit story.

"Liars always have a justification in their own minds. My first ex-wife said she lied about her cheating to save our marriage."

I sober on hearing this. "That sucks."

A sensation of tenderness for him envelops me. He must feel it too, the way his gaze softens, his lips open slightly, and his hands slide down from my wrists till our fingers intertwine. My insides ache with the desire to feel his arms tighten around me, pulling me close, pressing his lips against mine.

But before this happens, I don't know why, Mom's *liar, liar, pants on fire* echoes in my ears, breaking the mood for me. All at once, I hate myself for what I'm doing. Michael has already gone through the hell of a cheating wife who lied to him. How am I any different, lying about being divorced? Anthony and I have never even discussed divorce, for god's sake.

I didn't expect to care for Michael so much, so soon. I believed our connection could be short-lived, simple, uncomplicated. Up and down, in and out. A single act of copulation leaving us mutually satisfied, needing nothing more.

But it isn't like that, not for me, and not for him as far as I can tell. He even said fate had a hand in our meeting. *Fate.* The poor man thinks this is something real and true and preordained for god's sake. I can't... I just can't be with him under false pretenses, no different than plunging a treacherous sword through his trusting heart. I can't do it like this.

I rip my face away and pull back my hands. Horrible words escape my lips and pollute the air with their awfulness. "Thank you, I had a nice time. I'd love to invite you in for coffee but I have an early morning appointment tomorrow. I hope you understand."

A look of shocked confusion flashes in his face as he grasps for words. "Sure," he mutters.

I open my door and he simultaneously gets out from his side. We meet and hug briefly in the middle and wish each other good night. Turning toward the house, tears spring to my eyes as I try to unravel my feelings. When I signed up for online dating, I told myself the goal was a single night of glorious love-making, but now at the brink of that possibility, I pulled back. *Stupid, stupid woman*, I berate myself.

Ascending the stairs with clouded vision, I cling to the outer rail and fumble for my key at the landing. But then I'm not really surprised to find the door unlocked, another casualty of my fluster over Michael. I pause and look back to find him watching from inside the car, too much the gentleman to leave before ensuring I make it safely into the house. I wave to let him know all is well, although all is not the slightest bit well as I watch him drive away.

I enter and shut the door behind me, leaning against it, imagining his body crushed against mine, his tongue in my mouth, his... *stop it*, I tell myself, shaking off the sensation, throwing on the light. At once I get a different sort of feeling. Something is wrong inside my house, but I'm not sure what.

26

THE THEFT

There are too many lights on. I'm usually very careful to turn off all except the hall lamp and front porch light before I go out, a habit my thrifty mother instilled in me. But from where I stand, I can see light coming from the kitchen, the family room, and the upstairs hall. There's a small pile of dirt next to the mat. I always take off my shoes when I enter to avoid messes, and I'm pretty certain Michael's shoes were clean when he came in briefly before we went to the gala.

My senses snap into high alert but after a few seconds of straining for the sounds of an intruder, I've got zilch. Still, I take out my phone, wondering if it makes sense to call the police with such sketchy evidence of a possible home invasion. This becomes a moot point when it turns out I forgot to recharge my phone last night and now it's dead. Since I have to go inside anyway to plug it in, I may as well investigate myself.

Sadly, situations like these are when I need a man in my life. For the first time since I got here, I miss Anthony who for all his annoying qualities has always been the one to investigate things that go bump in the night. And why shouldn't he? Probably ninety-nine percent of intruders are male, and therefore who better to face them than another of their gender?

But tonight it falls to me to defend Mom's house and I'm frozen in indecision. Opening the door to peer back outside, my first sensation is disappointment over Michael not having returned to idle at my curb, wondering if I might have second thoughts about inviting him in. There are in fact no cars at all on the street out front, and wouldn't a thief need a getaway vehicle?

Something bangs in the house that makes my heart skip a beat until I remind myself the furnace makes noises like that all the time. After listening a moment longer for creaking floorboards without hearing anything, I decide against my better judgment to do my own investigating. Tiptoeing into the kitchen, I grab our largest knife, the one used for carving turkeys since I was old enough to remember. I brandish it ahead of me like it's an inadequate sword, while creeping from one room to another, poking into closets, whipping aside shower curtains, and peeking under beds. Once I'm sure I have the place to myself, I replace the carving knife, throw the front door bolt, and verify the back door is locked before collapsing on a chair with a sigh of relief.

I don't sit for long. It's still possible a burglar came here and stole something of value. Earlier I noticed my new mermaid weathervane lying in her box right where I left her, thank god. I would hate to lose what could be both the first and last gift I ever receive from Michael.

I begin a new search with the goal of identifying things that might have been taken, asking myself what I'd be looking to steal if I were in that line of work. Though bulky items would be tough to carry down the steps and likely to attract the attention of vigilant passersby, I do a quick round of accounting for all the TVs, computers, and other devices.

Moving on to Mom's desk, I find her checkbook resting in

its usual spot, and her files in the cabinet organized in what appears to be their usual order, not messed up in any way that would suggest someone rifled through them looking for credit card numbers or her social security card.

The family silver springs to mind, but the dining room drawer appears to hold the full set, minus the smattering of forks, knives and spoons that have been lost over the decades. Lastly, I check Mom's jewelry in her bedroom. The box is on the dresser along with two sterling silver picture frames displaying individual wedding portraits of her and Dad. From a brief glance in the crowded box, I'm pretty sure nothing has been taken because what thief would pick through it carefully? They'd toss the contents in a bag and get out of here fast.

Phew. I collapse on Mom's bed, exhaustion and disappointment overwhelming me, ready to fall asleep right here rather than trudge upstairs to my own room. But at the moment when I lower my head to her pillow, my brain flashes with the image of the one thing that is actually missing, and I can only wonder that I didn't think of it sooner, because it's of far greater value than any other item in the house.

27

MISSING MOTHER

I spring out of Mom's bed, fully alert again now. Without having any real idea what to do, I race back to the family room.

"Where's your box of ashes?" I ask the chair.

To my relief, she's still talking to me. *How should I know? You're the one who's supposed to be keeping track of me.*

"Who took them? Who was in the house?"

You got me. When you're not here, I'm nothing but a piece of furniture.

I can see I'm not going to get any help from this quarter. I could swear I left her box on the bed, but I don't know when I last noticed it there. Could I have moved it somewhere else without realizing, and without remembering afterwords? Considering I have daily conversations with my dead mother's chair, it's more than possible my mind is playing games with me.

I search the house yet again, starting in her bedroom and expanding outward to the rest of the first floor. Maybe I moved the box into a closet, a cupboard, or a drawer for safekeeping. I continue my search upstairs, checking cubbyholes I've not looked in since I got here, making sure I don't miss a single spot.

She's not here. I return to the family room to muse. "The door was unlocked, anyone could've entered and taken you."

I'm sure I'm worth a lot on the open market.

"There might be a market for intact corpses, but why would anyone want someone's ashes?"

They might think I have mystical properties. I bet I do.

"Like a good luck charm? Hmm, I doubt it. Most likely they were after that beautiful, sturdy box."

You're saying your mother's worth less than a box?

"Not to me. But someone else could use it as a jewelry box."

And yet they ignored a box with actual jewelry in it.

I return to Mom's bedroom and glance around, recalling how I loaded a large cardboard box for the thrift store just yesterday. Without thinking, could I have added Mom's remains to the giveaway pile? In fact, it might've happened almost any time in the last few weeks. I've been filling and delivering donation boxes every few days.

I've certainly had recent incidences when I do something I can't remember doing, though the evidence of my doing it is clearly in front of me. Maybe I'm getting Alzheimer's. I would have no idea, of course, and there isn't anyone living here with me to notice the changes in my behavior. I probably should make a doctor's appointment, although who really wants to know in advance if they're in the process of losing their mind.

I consider calling the police, but given their previous indifference over the case of the missing pretend-husband, I don't expect them to do anything. There's nothing to be gained from my losing any more sleep. With luck, the solution will come to me in the morning.

28

DETECTIVE WORK

I'm at the entrance of the Crystal Creek Thrift Store two minutes before opening. A nice woman around my own age opens the door for me. So far I'm the only customer.

I introduce myself and she tells me her name is Sally.

"I'm looking for a mahogany box about yay big." I indicate the size with my hands. "I didn't mean to give it away. It's a family heirloom." It's too embarrassing to reveal I may have accidentally donated my own mother.

"Anything inside the box?" she asks.

"Nothing but a ghost."

"Oh, you better find it. We wouldn't want the store to become haunted."

Together we scan the shelves, but it's nowhere to be found. "Must be in the back," Sally says. "Follow me."

Boxes are stacked high in the storage area. "Some of your donations should still be here," she says. "It can take days to get things sorted and moved out front. Feel free to look around."

"Thanks." I begin the laborious process of sifting through what they've got, while Sally returns to monitor the register at the front of the store.

An hour passes before I discover the most recent cardboard box I dropped off, still untouched. Unfortunately, Mom's box isn't inside. For two more hours I continue the search, finding many of my own donations, until I'm satisfied she isn't here. I don't believe anyone could've taken her home with them either. When someone buys a box they're going to check inside it, and surely the sight of Mom's remains—including bone fragments—would discourage even the most determined collector from going through with the purchase.

I return home with a heavy heart. Somebody stole Mom's box from the house; there's no other explanation. At the risk of being subject to ridicule, I make another phone call to the Windset Police Department and ask to speak with Detective Dempsey. At least a week has passed since I dropped by the station and filled out the annoying form.

"Has there been any progress on locating the man claiming to be my mother's husband?" I ask.

The detective launches into another of his rapid monologues. "We went to the restaurant and couldn't find anyone who knew him. He paid in cash so no credit card receipt. No one in the ambulance or the hospital questioned his identity, they just assumed he was her husband. The good news, your mom didn't pull a marriage certificate anywhere on the South Shore. Anything happening on your end? Anyone tried to use her credit cards?"

"The thief had plenty of time to use them before I cancelled them, but didn't." I cough. "Something did happen, though. My mother's gone missing."

"Was I wrong in thinking she was dead?"

"I had her ashes stored in a mahogany box. Now that's disappeared." I'm not sure, but the sound I hear may be the detective's smothered laughter.

"So you think the missing man who may be her hubby ran off with the missing remains of her?"

Until now, I had not even thought of that. "Yes. Is that so surprising?"

"Well we don't see a lot of stolen ashes cases around here, like I mean never, but the good news is it's a felony so we can prioritize the investigation."

"Oh really? A felony?"

"Any theft of human remains. Tell me when you last saw your mom I mean her box."

I give him the details of where I put it, when I recalled last seeing it, when I noticed it was gone, and where I've checked for it so far.

"You said the front door was unlocked?"

"Mm."

Thankfully he doesn't lecture me on the poor security around here. "Neighbors see anything?" he asks.

"Most the houses on our street only get used in the summer. Hardly anyone's around this time of year."

"Okay then we'll—"

"—I did see a man at Mom's viewing who acted really suspicious and ran away when I asked him who he was. He doesn't match the description of her so-called husband but I think he knows something. He drives a Mercedes with a Red Sox sticker, you know, the one with an actual pair of socks."

"Yeah we don't see too many of those stickers around here," he says.

"I'm not sure I appreciate your sarcasm, Detective."

"You home now?"

"Yes."

"We're comin' over to take some prints and talk to the neighbors if we can find any."

True to his word, Detective Dempsey arrives with an officer twenty minutes later. They search the house in case I misplaced the box, take prints off the door handles and other shiny surfaces, and even gather a sample of the dirt by the floor mat.

It wasn't easy to hold myself back from cleaning it first thing in the morning, and now I'm grateful for my restraint.

I already gave them photos of my mother, and now I have Billy at the funeral home text the police a picture of the cremation box. They leave to go interview anyone who didn't flee south for the season. At least the one positive thing that could come of all this is if Mom's ashes lead us to her mystery man.

29

ROSES

When the bell rings thirty minutes after the cops leave, I throw down my paintbrush and rush to answer the door, thinking they must have information. Instead, a flower delivery man hands me a box. "Viola Bluff?"

"Thank you!" I snatch the box from him and hurry into the kitchen to open it. "Michael sent me flowers!" I exclaim loudly enough for Mom's chair to hear me in the family room. I place the dozen gorgeous red roses in my mother's finest crystal vase before pausing to sniff their heavenly scent. "He must not be upset with me after all!"

I swirl the vase in my arms like it's him and we're waltzing our way to the table by the window in the family room. What a wonderful gesture after how I cut him off and sent him packing last night. What a powerful indication of the strong feelings he must have for me.

Inspired by the beautiful flowers, I'm about to continue work on my mural, when it occurs to me I should text him a picture of them along with my gushing thanks. But as I try to capture the best lighting, a call comes in from Anthony wanting to FaceTime.

I would normally ignore his call, except it's highly unusual for him to use FaceTime, probably because he's half-working on something else whenever he talks to me. Thinking he might have some news, possibly about our daughter, I dash into the kitchen to answer the phone while making sure he won't glimpse the roses Michael sent.

Anthony looks happy for a change. "Did you get the flowers?" he says.

I stare at him, stunned by his question, with a sudden dizziness overwhelming me. I grab onto the counter to steady myself.

"Are you all right?" he asks.

I struggle to find my voice. "Yeah," I croak. "I just got up too quickly."

"You got the roses, right?"

Part of me still wants to believe Michael sent them and Anthony somehow found out about them and is claiming credit. But I remember now that the delivery man used my married name whereas Michael only knows me by my maiden name. Anthony sent the flowers, not Michael. *Anthony.*

I throw on a fake smile. "Yeah, I did. They're beautiful. Thank you." I do my utmost to suppress the fury rising inside me. Anthony never gets me flowers, not for my birthday or after I've done something nice for him, or even on Valentine's Day. The only exception is when he knows I'm pissed off about something and wants to worm his way back into my good graces—an act of manipulation, not an apology.

"Can I see them?" he asks.

"Uh, sure. Hold on." I have to retrieve them from the family room so that Anthony doesn't see the mural. He'll be angry if he learns I've been "wasting my time" on that instead of spending every waking moment settling Mom's estate so that I can return to California as quickly as possible. I hurry back with the vase and set it on the kitchen table before showing it to him on FaceTime.

"Where were they?" He seems to be suspicious about everything these days, I can't imagine why.

"I had them in the family room so I can look at them while I organize Mom's stuff in there."

"What stuff are you organizing?"

"Does it really matter?"

"I guess not." I can tell he's struggling not to be annoying. "I wanted to congratulate you on your painting."

Max, that traitor child, must've told him. "Thanks."

"Why didn't you tell me about it? I had to find out from our daughter."

"I didn't think you'd be interested."

"That's not fair. I'm proud of you. It's pretty amazing you found time to do that with everything else going on over there."

Here we go. "It didn't take me long," I lie.

"Did anyone buy it at the exhibit?"

"I don't want to sell it. Not yet, anyway."

"Oh. I assumed the purpose was to bring in some extra money."

"I thought we were doing okay in that department," I say.

"Every little bit helps. Anyway, let's not dwell on that. There's something else I wanted to tell you that should make you happy. I've thought about what you said about Lopez." This was the contractor I wanted to get for the bathroom remodel. "His prices are high," Anthony continues, "but I looked at our finances, and we can afford it. It's fine with me if you want to hire him."

My stomach rumbles with discontent. "Sure," I say, realizing I've been using this word with Anthony a lot. "Sure" now means, "There's plenty I don't like about what you just said but it's too stressful for me to argue about it."

This is classic Anthony on full display. First off, I know he's now suspicious something is going on over here. He has a decent radar for that sort of thing, because something suspicious actually is going on. Chances are good Max mentioned my "old high school friend" Michael. Anthony would be certain the man had an unrequited yearning for me, even if Max said he and Cadence were all over each other. Since long ago when I first began dating my husband, he has worried about my reconnecting with high school and college beaus, as ridiculous as that sounds. Ironically, Anthony would never be able to imagine my going even farther and purposely setting out to meet a brand new, previously unknown man. This thought would blow his mind.

There is more to parse in this supposed concession of his. He thinks he's being magnanimous by allowing the contractor of my choice to be hired. And yet he is dumping the entire job on me as usual by telling me that "I" can hire him. A real concession would be for him to say, "I will call the contractor and deal with him myself." A statement like this would demonstrate an understanding of the heart of the problem, a level of self-knowledge that's eluded him for all our years of marriage. In other words, a statement like this would blow my mind.

"You don't sound very happy about it." Anthony expects meaningless concessions to be met with an outpouring of gratitude.

"I'm a little distracted at the moment." I consider telling him that Mom is missing, but just as quickly reject the notion. Instead of showing sympathy, he'll give me the third degree regarding why I left the door unlocked. I'm feeling guilty enough without him piling on more. I just want to get off the phone and return to my mural. "I've got an appointment with Mom's estate lawyer in an hour and I need to prepare some stuff first."

"Okay, I hope it goes well. Love you," he says.

"Sure."

After hanging up, I move the roses to Mom's bedroom so I won't have to spend the afternoon looking at them and feeling sorry for myself that Anthony sent them instead of Michael.

"These are for you," I say to her bed. "You liked him better than I do."

30

THE ONE THAT GOT AWAY

A week later Jackie calls at seven in the evening. "What are you doing tonight?"

I'm alone at home drinking my second glass of wine feeling sorry for myself, the same thing I've been doing every day since the art gala when I pushed Michael out of my life. It's pathetic.

Not wanting to go out in this mood, I say, "Watching a movie."

"Well screw that, you can watch Netflix any time. Come on down to The Jolly Taster. We're celebrating!"

"What are you celebrating?"

"Ken and I just got engaged!"

I can hear voices cheering in the background. "Congratulations! I thought you were done with marriage though."

"So did I, till I met Ken. Come drink a toast to us. You might recognize some other people here."

I glance around the family room, which now looks positively dreary. I've left dirty dishes on the tables. Shelves I've picked over are half-empty. Boxes are overflowing with junk on the floor. The mural, which I stopped working on a few days ago, just looks like someone threw a bucket of paint at the wall. It's pathetic.

"Fine. I'm coming," I say. How can I refuse? For whatever it's worth, I owe my recent success at art to her.

"Be quick!" she says.

I take her advice to heart because people our age have a tendency to go to bed early. I throw on the outfit I bought at Anthropologie, even though wearing it without Michael almost seems like cheating. A quick brush of the hair, wash of the face, and smearing of lipstick and I'm off.

The Jolly Taster is booming. Seems like this must be the happening place for the forty-plus crowd. People with some money to spend, because it looks like fancy wines paired with tiny plates of food.

"Vi, over here!" Jackie shouts.

I wind my way around the bar to where her group mingles at the far end of it. Ken must've wandered off, but I hug and congratulate Jackie.

"You remember Skipper?" she shouts.

She pulls forward a guy who looks like Jerry Garcia, with shoulder-length frizzy hair, a bushy beard, and aviator sunglasses though we're not outside and it's nighttime anyway. He even has on a Grateful Dead T-shirt.

"Where you been all my life, Sagey?" He crushes me in his arms, overpowering me with the cloying stench of weed.

Skipper is the only one who ever called me *Sagey*, from my last name, *Sagewood*. "Lost," I tell him, because it's how I feel these days.

"Hallelujah, now you're found. Jesus, Sage. Last time I saw you, you were stoned out of your gourd swaying around to Led Zeppelin."

"Oh come on, that could've been any of us."

"Truth. We got the best weed back then, none of this crap they're selling now. Remember that time we smoked at JD's house, then went out on his parents' Whaler and capsized it? Man, that was epic." Skipper does not appear to have changed since our high school years, when he was famous for being a stoner dude. I don't remember his actual name, but everyone called him *Skipper* because he always insisted on steering whatever boat we got our hands on, even after he totaled three of them.

I admit I was infatuated with him one summer, and there was even a week or so when he called me his girlfriend, but it ended after I realized he was very much a *love the one you're with* kind of guy. He always talked a lot. Seems like he still does.

"Viola?" another man says behind me.

I turn away from Skipper and recognize the guy I met at the art show who owns a gallery.

"Tucker Hanwell." He gives me a hug like we know each other better than we do.

"Hi, nice to see you again."

He takes my arm and draws me into a quieter spot in the corner. I glance back at Skipper, who's already talking to another woman at the bar.

"Can we discuss your painting?" Tucker says.

"Uh, sure."

Jackie, in passing, thrusts a glass of red wine into my hand. "Drink up, kiddo." She moves on before I can thank her.

"I was wondering if you might want to do a series about your mother?"

"My mother?" I don't remember mentioning her. I said the chair was about getting my tooth pulled.

"Jackie told me about your trauma. Your mother sleeping with your ex-husband?"

That big mouth. But at least she relegated Anthony to an *ex-*.

"She thought I already knew," he defends her.

I swill my wine. This conversation probably calls for it. I've already had two large glasses at home, so I'm feeling it. Which is kind of the effect I want right now.

"Have you spoken to a therapist?"

I suppose I should be annoyed, but I suddenly feel myself wanting to open up about it. "No, but I should. I mean, what the hell? How would you feel if you learned your father slept with your wife before you knew her and then never told you about it until he was dead?"

"Well my ex-wife actually slept with my bloody brother, but yes, I guess a father would've been worse. Except after our divorce she married my brother so now I've lost both of them."

"Oh man, I'm sorry."

"I just wanted you to know I get it. It would make some powerful art. A set of paintings analyzing your feelings about your mother. And your ex. Like a memoir in art."

"Yeah. I can see it." I chug some more wine.

A dinging of spoon against glass begins. "Hey everybody," Skipper calls out. "Everybody, let's drink a toast to the beautiful young couple that just got engaged. Congrats, Jackie and Ken!"

"Congrats!" we all shout. I chug the rest of my glass and before I know it, Tucker is handing me another. "My wife was fifteen years younger than me," he says. "That's why I only date older women now." He gives me a pointed look. At least he's not pretending that he thinks I'm younger than I am.

"Older women have it all together. They've run households. Some have run businesses. You don't have to take care of them. They take care of everything."

Jackie and Ken are wrapped in a celebratory kiss. I'm happy for them. Online dating worked for them. Who knows if it will last, but at this age it's best to concentrate on the present. Feeling great about ourselves today? Good enough.

Tucker is pressing closer to me. "I like you, Viola. We share similar trauma."

My hand feels unsteady and fearing I'll drop my glass, I

lower it to the counter. When I look up, Tucker is coming at me with lips parted and suddenly we're kissing. Kissing! *Why couldn't this be Michael?* When I pull back from him, he relents.

"I wasn't expecting that."

"Too soon?" he says.

"Can you excuse me?" My head is spinning as I make my way toward the exit.

Skipper appears next to me. "What are you doing after this?"

"Going home and reading a good book." This is a lie. I'm too drunk to read.

"No, seriously, you wanna grab a late dinner?"

Seriously, I don't. "I can't, I'm tired."

"How about tomorrow? You have any idea how sorry I was to hear you moved to California? I had a thing for you. You were the one that got away," Skipper says.

The back of my mind is trying to process what he's telling me. I never thought I might be someone's *one that got away*. Nor did I ever imagine an old high school beau would have any interest in me now. There was a time when interest from Skipper would have sent my heart soaring.

"I'm still married," I tell Skipper.

"I have a girlfriend but we're not like, committed."

Same old Skipper.

"Good night," I say.

But as I emerge into the cold night air and breathe deeply, my head clears. Michael preferred me to Cadence. Tucker wanted to kiss me. Skipper thinks I'm the one that got away. And I'm sixty-three.

Falling into an easy stride, I pass a group of twenty and thirty-year-old women heading into the bar. I raise a cocky eyebrow at them. *Beat that, suckers.*

31

EYE OF THE STORM

In the morning I call Michael despite being unsure whether he'll ever speak to me again.

To my happiness, he picks up on the third ring. "Hello, Viola." Though it's a tentative greeting like he's not sure what to expect from me, the sound of his voice still comforts me.

I get right to the point. "I'm sorry for the other night. I'm not sure what came over me."

"I'm really glad you called. I was trying to give you time... and space. I almost called you five times since then."

"That's so sweet. This is all new to me. It's not that I regret anything."

"I get it. It's hard when a relationship ends, even if that's what you want."

I've resolved to tell him the truth, but not over the phone. I owe it to him to tell him in person and to bravely accept the consequences. "How would you feel about getting dinner tonight?"

He sounds a little surprised, but warmly accepts the invitation. He insists he'll pick me up at my house.

When he shows up early again, there's a moment of awkwardness until he smiles, which instantly puts me at ease. I don't know how he does it, but he has this look like he sees right into me, like he understands who I am at my center without my having to say anything.

"Would you like to see the house this time?" I ask.

"I'd love to. Are you looking for my professional opinion of it?"

"I see what you're doing. Okay. I would appreciate that."

As I lead him from room to room, he admires the structure, the layout, and the custom features like built-in bookshelves. Listening to him, I have an idea that feels like a revelation. The way I've been obsessing over my wrinkles and sagging and all the symptoms of old age—it turns out I've been looking at the older parts of the house the same way. His praise reminds me to value the signs of a long life well-lived, whether it's a home or a human being. Surviving this many years takes good bones and fortitude.

These sage thoughts float through my brain as we enter Mom's bedroom and suddenly I see the dozen roses where I deposited them on her dresser. One would have to be blind not to notice these glorious flowers in full bloom, and Michael is not blind. He narrows his eyes in my direction. "Roses?" he says.

"For Mom." I attempt a casual tone.

"That's unusual for a death."

"There was no card. It must've been her mystery date."

"Ah."

I get a fluttery sensation inside thinking he's jealous that I might have another suitor. I leave the possibility floating in the air as I lead him to the family room next.

He pauses beside me in front of the mural. "What's it going to be?" he asks.

"It's a work in progress." I've only just begun painting the rock that the ship will crash into. Most of it is just sea and sky at the moment, but I have so much more planned. I pick up my sketchpad. "This is roughly what I'm imagining, so far." It shows the ship crashing against the rock.

"A demon chair and now a massive shipwreck? Where will your imagination go from here?"

"Meteor strike? I don't know. Do you think I'm nuts? It might be hard to sell the house with a mural of a shipwreck. Some people might consider it bad karma."

"You know what I think?"

"I think you're about to tell me."

"This shows you don't want to sell the house. You can't, with your beautiful mural inside. What if the buyers don't appreciate art? It would be a crime if they painted over it."

"This is *Da Seat*, by the way." I point at her chair. "Though her ashes are gone, her spirit remains."

"Nice to meet you, Mrs. Da Seat. In real life, you aren't scary at all."

"That was just a flight of my imagination. In real life, we get along quite well."

"You can hear her talk?"

"You can't?"

"Not yet."

I like this implication that he plans to keep trying. "Thanks for looking at the house, but let's not discuss it now. That would feel too much like work. We should relax and have fun tonight."

When we step out onto the landing, we both notice a change in the weather. I shiver and fasten the top button of my coat.

"Wind's out of the northeast," Michael says.

These are ominous words in this part of the country. "The temperature's dropped."

"The forecast shows a storm coming in by morning. Fingers crossed it's not too bad."

Twenty minutes later we're staring at a sign outside the restaurant: "Power outage. Closed till further notice."

Snow begins falling. A few light flakes settle on Michael's head. "Any ideas for another restaurant?" he says.

"Do you want to come back to my place?" arises from my mouth before I consider the possible consequences. "Then we don't have to worry about driving back after the snow has piled up."

"I don't suppose you have any leftover make-believe beef wellington or baked Alaska?"

"There's an unlimited supply but it's not terribly satisfying. Whatever real food I have is pretty random. Are you game?"

The snowfall thickens during the twenty minute drive back to where we started. We step into two inches of snow getting out of the car and the icy wind whips our faces. I know I should suggest to Michael that he head back home immediately before he ends up stuck at my place for the night, but I can't get myself to do it. I sent him packing the last time he was here; this time, the decision is up to him.

We go straight to the kitchen where I check the fridge and cupboards. I've already used or thrown out much of the food that was here when I arrived. However, I discover some of the items I bought during the food-Anthony-hates shopping trip. My hopes brighten as I remember what I baked this very morning. "Cornbread?" I ask.

"Love it."

"With a side of scrambled eggs and baked beans?"

"Mouth-watering. What can I do?"

"Make yourself at home."

He ignores my advice and finds jobs for himself. The man sets the table, microwaves the beans, locates and opens a bottle of a chardonnay, and pours out a generous serving for me. All I manage in that time is scrambling the eggs.

"I don't get why any woman would divorce you," I say when we're settled with our humble meal at the table. "You're Mr. Perfect. Not only do you do stuff, but you figure out what needs doing."

He makes a scoffing sound. "If you only knew."

"Honestly, I'm a little intimidated by the standards you set."

He pats his lips with his napkin and clears his throat. "Maybe it's time for full disclosure."

"You're frightening me." But at the same time, I'm hoping he has a few bad boy exploits in his past to balance my own crappy behavior.

"You know I'm an alcoholic, right? As unbelievable as it sounds, I didn't realize that till I nearly killed myself when I was in my mid-twenties."

"What happened?"

"I drank myself into oblivion, got in a car, and drove into a very large tree at three am in a remote area. I'm only alive today because I was lucky enough that another driver saw me veer off the road and called the ambulance that arrived before I bled out."

I swallow heavily at the thought of him losing his life.

"As soon as I recovered, I started going to AA meetings and gave up drinking pretty quickly. Everything changed about my attitude toward life. I mean, I no longer felt immortal like young people do. You can die in an instant and it might not even be your own bad judgment that caused it. The thought that I could've crashed into another car and killed some blameless soul, god forbid a child, bothered me even more than the possibility of killing myself. Death is random and can take anyone at any time. Sorry, I know this is depressing."

"You still haven't said anything to change my mind about you being Mr. Perfect right now."

"Oh, we're getting there. When I realized there was no guarantee I'd still be alive from one day to the next, I started making quick decisions."

"That sounds like a good thing."

"I'm not so sure. Sometimes when you make fast decisions, you make the wrong decisions. I did it four times in fact. I'm talking about my marriages."

"Four?" My internet search unveiled only two.

"Yup."

"I thought only movie stars had that many. You're not still married to them, are you?"

"God no. One at a time was hard enough."

"What was wrong with them?"

He laughs. "Kind of you not to ask what was wrong with *me*. My first had to deal with my alcoholism. She did so by cheating on me, but it's hard to blame her. Once after a blackout I woke up in bed with two women. I had no idea who they were or what went on the night before. Am I still Mr. Perfect?"

"Tell me about number two."

"A whirlwind wedding. Happened so fast I barely knew the bride. She was managing a sales department when we got together, but quit after we married and showed no interest in ever working again. Problem is, she didn't do anything around the house either. I got sick of doing everything for both of us."

Shades of Anthony. But at least he brings in a paycheck.

"I'm not even sure why number three married me. She actually loved her job, worked long hours, and spent the rest of her time hanging out with her large group of friends. I hardly ever saw her. A year after we married, it was over."

"And for the grand finale...?"

"I got her pregnant and wanted to do the right thing. I hoped we would grow into our relationship, but it was always a struggle. Our personalities and temperaments were so different. The year our second graduated college, I filed for divorce. When she got the papers, she said 'Hallelujah.'

"You can call me Mr. Imperfect now."

"I'm relieved," I say. "It's hard to live up to perfection. We're both human. Please don't forget that."

"I can't wait for your disclosures."

"My representative will drop them off next week."

"I'm not letting you off that easy," he says. "But first a visit to the bathroom."

I'm feeling nervous, but now that Michael has opened up to me, I'm determined to do the same for him. Weirdly, it doesn't actually bother me that he's had four wives. That's no worse than having a single husband who you haven't really much liked for years, and yet you pathetically hang onto him hoping something will change. At least Michael had the sense to recognize when things weren't working.

Outside, the force of the wind is rattling the place. I take out my phone, planning to check the storm forecast but I get distracted by a text from JetBlue. Why are they messaging me when I don't have any flights reserved? But on reading it, I discover the intended recipient was Anthony. Since he never arranges his own travel, I have the notifications on his account set to my phone. According to JetBlue, Anthony's flight—a red eye to Boston tonight—has been slightly delayed.

I can feel my eyes bugging out of their sockets. *What the hell?* Anthony has booked his own flight to Boston and not said a word to me about it. He must be planning to surprise me, which can only mean one thing—he's overwhelmed by suspicion about what is going on here in his absence.

"Everything okay?" Michael says from behind me.

An electric spasm shoots through me and I flick my phone to a different window praying Michael hasn't seen the message. "Yeah, fine. Just checking the weather." I open the weather app.

"This storm is getting bigger." But Anthony's flight not getting cancelled tells me it's not as big as I need it to be.

"I saw you have storm windows. We should close them," Michael says.

My mind is racing. Anthony's flight arrives at six am. If he gets an Uber, he'll be here by 7:30. I can't let Michael stay the night and wake up in the morning to Anthony brewing our coffee. Not that he ever makes the coffee.

Even if I manage to send Michael home tonight without offending him again, how can I get rid of my husband as quickly as possible? If he sticks around for a while, how can I put a pause on my developing relationship with Michael without causing him to wonder what the hell is going on? And how will I explain to Anthony that I've been working on a mural instead of getting the repairs needed to put the house on the market? The mounting panic sends a shiver up my spine.

Through the window, I glimpse snow dropping in clumps outside. A gust of wind causes a loose shutter to bang against the house.

"Storm windows?" he repeats.

"Mm." He's right, they need to be lowered and I'm not sure I can manage the job by myself. Thank god he just revealed himself as a flawed person or I would feel even worse about making use of his builder skills before telling him he has to leave.

"Are they automatic?"

"Yeah, Mom didn't want them 'cause, you know, expensive, but I convinced her about ten years ago after a big nor'easter."

The lights flicker like the electric might go out, but then they stay on. Michael and I exchange a look that says, we better work fast. "Switches are by the windows. I'll do upstairs," I say.

"Better take a flashlight."

"Got my phone." I hear his footsteps cross the hall as I mount the creaky stairs to the second floor. From outside, a symphony of noises assaults us: wind whistling through gaps, loose shutters rattling, and frenzied waves smacking the shoreline. It's like Mother Nature is screaming at us.

Unfortunately, the process isn't quick. For a reason I can't recall, you have to hold down the switch until the storm window is fully closed. I finish the two in my bedroom and one in the bathroom and am just heading into the study when the lights flicker again and then go out.

After a few seconds pass, Michael shouts up from downstairs. "Any chance you have a generator?"

"If you mean one that works, then no." I blame myself. It broke down at the end of last winter season and Mom said she'd get it repaired by fall. But I never followed up with her, and only found out after she died that nothing had been done.

I turn on my phone flashlight and come downstairs. Michael is in the kitchen lighting candles.

"I took the liberty of going through the cupboards to find them."

"It's not taking a liberty when it's an essential activity."

"Any chance you know where the crank handle is for the storm windows?"

I flash my light into the corners of the utility closet. "Unless it looks like a mop, it isn't here. But here's a nice electric lantern."

"Any other thoughts where it might be?"

"Yeah."

"I'll get a fire going in the wood stove while you look."

I check the front hall closet next, followed by Mom's closet in her bedroom. I find it stored next to her ironing board.

"Success." I hold it up like it's Gandalf's staff.

Glancing up from arranging logs, Michael smiles.

"How about we change jobs?" I say. "I can build a fire. There's two windows in the study upstairs that aren't done."

Michael heads off with the lantern while I add kindling and

crumpled newspaper. Mom must've been one of the last people in the nation to still get home delivery.

When he returns I've got the fire going. "Can you check the local roads while I finish up down here? I want to see if we can get through to my apartment." he says.

"We?" I'm glad he's taking the initiative making plans to leave, but soon enough I'll have to make it clear I'm staying put.

"You shouldn't stay here. I'm not on the water. It'll be safer. Sorry, I don't mean to presume. I've got a guest bedroom."

I look up road conditions and it's not good. "Route 3 is closed."

"Crap," he says.

"I'll check the back roads."

"Don't bother. If it's so bad the highway's closed, it's not safe to drive anywhere."

"There's a spare bed in the study upstairs," I say before I can stop myself. I can't let the poor man perish outside in the blizzard. I have all night to think of an excuse to get him out of the house by 7:30 am. "Do you know this place withstood the blizzard of '78? There were like a hundred homes demolished, one of them right next door. And afterwards, Mom and Dad had our posts fortified."

"Good. You really don't mind if I stay?"

"I wouldn't make my worst enemy go out in this."

He smiles. "I better finish the storm windows."

My phone pings telling me I have a text message, making my stomach clench at the remembrance that Anthony's on his way here.

"Everything okay?" Michael pauses on his way to Mom's bedroom.

"It's just... my daughter. She saw the weather forecast. Making sure I'm okay." Here I go with the lies again.

"Nice kid." He leaves the room.

The text is actually from Jet Blue. *Good news.* Anthony's

flight is being diverted to Newark. At last a stroke of luck. It won't be easy for him to arrange another flight to Boston in the morning, with this weather system. Might be days before he can get here. I feel like doing cartwheels across the family room floor. *Weee! We're gonna have a sleepover.*

I'm about to head upstairs to put sheets on the spare bed when a new thought occurs. I hurry to the front door and when I open it, a wind blast nearly knocks me over.

"Whoa, what're you doing?" Michael approaches behind me.

"I just realized... we need to move the cars. When the tide rises, it'll get flooded down there."

"I'll do it," he says.

"We both need to do it."

He doesn't argue. We bundle back into our boots and jackets before heading out. Wind-driven snow stings our faces while the noise of the tempest deafens us. We take baby steps to the landing below, cautious of the snow and ice.

At the street level, there's not much accumulation, probably because the wind's coming from the sea and blowing the snow westward. I hurry into Mom's car while Michael climbs into his SUV. At first the Cadillac doesn't seem as if the engine will start, but after three tries, it thankfully comes to life. Michael waits while I reverse out of my parking spot, then shift to low gear to move forward down the street. I take the first left, but as the grade rises, so does the height of the snowfall. I make it about twenty feet from the intersection before the car slides, the wheels spin, and I'm no longer moving forward. I gently pump on the brake and the car shudders to a stop. It's not going anywhere else tonight.

Just as I'm about to open my door, I notice movement next to the shrubs by the side of the house nearest me. I'm startled to recognize the coyote that I dubbed *Signal*. The poor thing looks miserable covered in snow, watching me. I glance inside the car, wondering if there's anything here that would help him, but aside from letting him into the car to warm up, there's nothing to offer. Back at the house, I have those doggie treats I bought, and it's tempting to run back and fetch them, but I know it's never good to feed wild animals. All I can do is send him my best wishes. *Stay warm, stay safe, sweet Signal.*

When Michael pulls up in the SUV behind me, Signal takes off up the road away from us, his paws sinking into the powdery snow with each step. I lose sight of him as Michael emerges from his car. I get out too and meet him midway.

"Did you see the coyote?" I shout over the din.

"No."

"Poor thing looks frozen."

"Nothing we can do."

I don't argue. "My car won't go any further. We'll have to leave it here."

"It's fine, nobody else is going to drive this way tonight."

A sudden gust blows off my hood and stirs up my hair. Michael holds a heavy-duty flashlight that he must've had in his car and lights our way. We go as fast as we're able, trudging through snow halfway up our calves until we reach the house. The cold and wet seeps into my boots, reminding me these things are more decorative than functional.

We help each other back up the steps and through the door before slamming it behind us with relief. Looking at each other —soaked and wind-blown—makes us laugh. We strip off our outerwear, leaving it to form a puddle in the entry.

I haven't forgotten that at this very moment, Anthony is on his way to Boston by way of Newark. I'm also very conscious of not having told Michael about my marriage.

But this is the moment when I decide, if he's willing, that I will sleep with him tonight. All the reasons circle my brain like ponies on a carousel. Because when I saw Michael the first time after he intercepted my polar plunge, I felt a connection as if we had met before. Because the dating site insisted on bringing his profile to my attention afterward. Because he is handsome and sexy and clever and kind and funny and all those things I would be so lucky to have in a lover. Because there will come a time—*not now*—when I'll have to confess my lies and I'm unsure of the effect they will have on him. Because Anthony will be here tomorrow and then, one way or another, I will be forced to deal with him. Because Signal the coyote granted us a rare visit, just now, outside my house, and this means all the signs have come together to form the eye of the perfect storm that is my life.

32

TAKE ME

In the family room, Michael lays another log on the fire and I pile our outerwear next to the wood stove hoping it will dry everything out by early morning. Fresh flames leap up as I lean close, rubbing my hands to warm them.

"Let's get you dry clothes," I say looking up at him.

I lead the way to my father's old closet in my parents' bedroom. Mom never threw out Dad's old things. Michael takes a lightly used T-shirt and a pair of boxers from a package that was never opened, along with Dad's bathrobe.

"You can wash and change in the upstairs bathroom," I tell him. "I'll use this one."

As he heads out of the bedroom, I'm praying he swallows a pill if he needs one. *Whatever it takes, baby.*

I strip in my parents' bathroom, take a speedy shower in order not to use all the remaining hot water, and put on one of Mom's silk slips. I top this with her fuzzy red robe so as not to announce my intentions too loudly when I join Michael.

After grabbing candles and matches, I use my phone flashlight to make my way up the steps. When I reach my bedroom, I find Michael has already lit several candles and is in the process of pouring me another glass of chardonnay. My first glimpse of him dressed in nothing but the shirt and boxers makes my heart go pitter patter.

"How did you know I would want more wine?"

"A wild guess."

"I brought extra candles," I say, laying my supply on the top of the dresser.

As he moves toward the door, I grasp his arm. "Will you stay with me?"

His gaze softens. I raise my hands to his shoulders, ignoring the niggling fear I've read him all wrong and he just wants to be friends.

To my delight, he meets me halfway, draws me close, and gives me a long, gentle kiss.

It isn't till now I remember I'm post-menopausal and can no longer make love without lube. With a major lack of foresight, I didn't bring any from California. Back then, I wasn't expecting to cheat on Anthony. "I'll be right back," I tell Michael before heading back to Mom's bathroom with the desperate hope that she has some, or if not exactly sexual lubricant, something with similar qualities. I'm even thinking Vick's Vaporub might do the trick, with the added benefit of clearing our nasal passages.

My prayers are answered when I search her cupboards and discover an unopened bottle of actual lube. I hiss "y-e-s-s-s-s" like I just nailed my gymnastics routine, but then I can't help wondering if Mom had plans to sleep with her restaurant date —her "husband"—the night she died. I push the sad thought of her unfulfilled frolic from my head. Despite the nor'easter bearing down on us, I hope for only joyful thoughts tonight.

Upstairs I find Michael sitting in my bed with his chest bare and the sheet pulled up to his waist. The borrowed T-shirt and boxers are on the desk across the room. *He's not wasting time.* He watches as I set the lube on the bedside table and makes me laugh with a smug look of *I see I'm about to get laid.* I hang my robe on the hook behind the door and pause wondering if I should remove my slip in front of him or force him to somehow get it off of me when I'm lying in the bed. I wish he had not lit so many candles and wonder if he'd mind if I blew them out. But because I vowed to be brave tonight, I leave them flickering as I lift the silk slip over my head and let it float to the floor. It's too late to change anything about my wrinkly, saggy self, and therefore I refuse to allow myself to obsess over it. *This is me, here I am, take me or leave me.*

"You're beautiful," he says. He even looks and sounds like he means it.

He raises the covers for me to slide in beside him.

"Well, good night," he says, rolling the other way.

"Sweet dreams. See you in the morning." This is me calling his bluff.

A second later he turns back, raises himself over me, and presses his lips against mine. He looks at me with half-lidded eyes all the while he kisses me, and this more than anything gets my heartbeat racing. *He sees me, he desires me.* It's strange and comforting and electrifying to be in the arms of a man who makes me shudder with the want of him.

"I feel like a teenager having sex for the first time," I tell him, though I'm not sure if the sudden burst of heat rushing through me came from lying flesh to flesh or a hot flash.

"Except we skipped the furtive fumbling with hooks and buttons and zippers," he says.

"And no parents to arrive home unexpectedly so that one of us has to hide in the closet."

"I never felt so relaxed."

"Shit!" I shout over a spasm in my calf. "Cramp!" I push him aside so I can leap out of bed.

"You okay?"

"Need to walk it off."

The second my muscle unclenches, I slip back into his

arms. We get things going again, until another errant move has Michael groaning this time. "My back… it's okay… it's okay." But he doesn't look okay.

A few adjustments and we resume. "We've got this," Michael whispers to reassure me. When we catch each other's gaze, we burst out laughing.

"We're so freaking old," I say.

"We just need more lube." He reaches for the bottle.

"Oh yeah. Put it everywhere."

"I love your breasts."

"Your whiskers are hot."

We move in sync.

"You must've done this before," he says.

"Not like this."

We respond to what seems to bring each other the most pleasure and get a real rhythm going.

"Oh baby," he says. "That's the way."

My god, this is heaven, I'm having sensations I haven't felt in years. Things speed up and soon we're banging toward an incredible climax when *oh my fucking god,* I cry out in glorious exaltation, and seconds later he's right there with me and I'm already wondering if we could go for another when there's a loud cracking noise and all of a sudden the bed drops out from under us and Michael crashes down on me.

"We broke the fucking bed!" His face beams with pride.

"We've still got it, sweetheart."

33

ALARM

The persistent sound of an alarm wakes me. There's a light flashing from where I left my phone across the room, and aside from that, pitch darkness. A barrage of noise comes from outside. It takes me a second to recall where I am and what the hell is going on. *Michael.* Amazingly, despite the ruckus, he's still sleeping beside me on the mattress, which we moved off the broken frame onto the floor.

The alarm stops and I get a silly grin on my face remembering what we did last night. What I most want to do is throw myself on top of him and go another round.

But I need to find out what that alarm was. The candles have all gone out and the power hasn't returned. I can't tell if it's still nighttime or if we're halfway into tomorrow with all the storm windows down blocking any possible illumination.

Forcing my naked self out from under the covers, I shiver as I fumble my way to where I left my bathrobe. I check my phone —it's 3:16 am—and discover what caused all the buzzing and flashing. Last year I signed up for Windset alerts and just now I received a notification calling for the evacuation of everyone in this neighborhood.

"Michael, wake up. We have to get out of here."

The house shakes as a mighty swell slams against the side of it.

"Viola?" His voice is groggy with sleep.

"We're being evacuated. I'm checking the tide." I look it up online. "High tide in twenty minutes... correction... extra high tide in twenty minutes."

Another wave pounds the back wall.

"What time is it?" he says, sounding considerable more alert already.

When I tell him, he groans. Then he flings off the covers and my gosh, he's still naked. He flicks on the flashlight he left on the floor by the bed and gives me an eyeful as he searches for his shirt and boxers that somehow also landed on the floor. While he pulls them on, I envy how comfortable he seems in his own skin.

Michael clomps downstairs to retrieve the rest of his clothes that have hopefully dried by the fire, while I change into a warm outfit. Meanwhile the waves keep battering us and I'm wondering how much this house can tolerate before breaking into a pile of splinters. I should've thought of this much sooner, but there's stuff in here I want to save.

When I join him on the first floor, I find Michael putting on his boots like he's ready to go.

"I need to take some things to the car," I say.

"What things?"

"What if the house gets destroyed? There's Mom's documents... her jewelry... the family silver... her photo albums."

"What about your stuff?"

I stare at him dumbly until I recall I'm supposed to have been living here for a year. "Most of that's in storage for now." Sounds as reasonable as any of my other fabrications.

Before this day is out, I must tell him everything.

Another wave smacks the place so hard, a dish falls from a kitchen shelf and shatters on the floor.

"Let me check how deep the flooding is down there." He reaches for his jacket.

"Be careful."

When he opens the door, a gust knocks his hood off. He battles the wind to reach the landing and forces the door shut behind him.

Light is needed if I'm to find anything in here, but I don't want to light the candles again in case they get knocked over and start a fire. The house is probably too drenched for that, but I'm not taking chances. I turn on the electric lantern and all the flashlights I rounded up last night.

Michael fights off the gale like it's an invisible entity as he makes his way back into the house. He's soaking wet from head to toe. "We can't take anything from here. Too hard to carry. The water's up to my ass already, and every minute a new wave crashes over the seawall."

I tell myself not to worry. The house is a survivor. Mom's stuff will be fine. But we need to leave... just in case.

"Let me fill my backpack," I say.

"What can I do?"

"Get bags from the kitchen."

We race around the house gathering essentials. In the end, I have to make the tough decision to leave everything behind except our wallets, the keys to his SUV and Mom's car, our phones, Mom's most valuable jewelry, and a change of clothes wrapped tightly in a plastic bag for each of us. Documents can be replaced though it will be a royal pain to do so. My laptop files are backed up in the cloud.

"You ready?" Michael asks. "The surf is insane. We're gonna need a boat soon."

"Just one more thing."

He follows me back to the family room, where I raise the lantern above Mom's chair. Now more than ever I lament the loss of her remains. "I failed you, Mom. I promised you a sea burial."

She says nothing to relieve my guilt. A providential wave arrives and bangs the shutters so hard, a window cracks. I look back at the chair and inspiration strikes. I know what I have to do.

34

THE CHAIR

I grab Mom's chair by the arms and pull her toward me.

"What are you doing?" Michael says.

"You're going to think I'm bonkers."

"I knew there was that danger when I first saw you halfway into the freezing ocean."

"I promised I'd bury Mom's ashes at sea but they're gone now and I'll probably never get them back."

"And that's related because...?"

I give the chair another yank. "This chair probably contains more of her DNA than anything else remaining of her. She sat here for something like thirty years. It's amazing the thing didn't disintegrate. She sweat on it. Her hair dropped onto it. Her skin flaked on it. She drooled into it during her naps. She even bled on it."

"Did someone stab her?"

"Oh you know, paper cuts and leaky scabs. The sort of thing when you don't even notice you're bleeding."

"Didn't anyone ever clean it?"

"Does it look like it's been cleaned? Please, can you help me here?" I move to one side of the chair and try lifting it. It's a lot heavier than I thought.

"Viola. I get how painful this must be for you. I'd do anything to be able to help. But the water's too deep. We can't get this chair to the Lexus. Not sure it would fit anyway."

"I don't want to bring it to your car."

"But if the house survives this storm—and it probably will —so will the chair."

"You don't get it. This is as much Mom as the box of ashes. If I can't give them a sea burial, then it has to be the chair. Can you lift that side and help me carry it to the kitchen door?"

He stares at me. "Are you telling me the plan is to toss the chair out the back?"

"We don't have much time. The tide will go down soon."

"You're bonkers."

"I warned you." My plan is brilliant though. I mean, I don't think people in general are allowed to sink chairs at sea, so I wouldn't be able to charter a boat to take me out there and dump it.

He goes to the other side and lifts it. "Lucky for you, I'm a sucker for ridiculous schemes."

If I were not already head over heels with this man, now would be the moment.

Together we move her into the kitchen, with some struggle through the opening from the family room. We lower her again when we reach the back door.

"We have to time this well," Michael says. "Between waves."

"I know. I just need a moment."

He takes a second to realize I mean a moment alone with my mother. He steps out of the kitchen.

I rub the side of the chair with its soft velour covering. "This is it, Mom. The start of your next adventure.

I'm frightened.

This thought brings tears to my eyes. "There's nothing to be afraid of. Every human being has made this same journey before you, including your own husband and son. You can do this."

I'll miss you.

"Let's hope there's no missing in the next life. Back here, I'll be missing you like crazy."

I love you to the end of time and space.

"Me too, Mom. Me too." I touch my forehead to the place where hers used to rest. "Godspeed." I turn toward the family room. "Ready for you, Michael."

He returns and puts his arm around me. Pulls me close and kisses the side of my head. "You're a good daughter."

His words cause a melting inside me. I can't remember anyone ever telling me this before.

A wave pummels the wall, shaking us. "Now, before the next one!" I throw open the inner door, then the storm door. We grab the chair and through sheer orneriness, haul it to the outside, pushing and shoving it through the narrow opening.

"Back inside!" Michael shouts. We dash back and slam the storm door shut a second before the next wave lands.

Then I'm outside again with Michael right behind me. Each of us grabs an arm like she's an actual person, and we dash with her to the railing. With high tide, the water level is up to the top of the sea wall directly below us. I can see the next wave approaching and it's a beast.

I don't know where the strength comes from, though it might be akin to a case Mom told me about many years ago, of a mother lifting a car off her son who was pinned under it. Together we raise the ponderous chair and heave it over the deck rail into the roiling sea below. The next wave follows us as we dive for the back door and slide through together. With a second to spare, Michael kicks the door shut behind us and keeps his foot pressed against it as a wall of water hammers the frame. In the calm that follows, Michael flings his arms protectively around me. We're both trembling from our narrow escape. I felt certain that last one would scoop us up and carry us straight out to sea after the chair.

But we're safe inside for the moment. I latch the storm door, then Michael bolts shut the inner door. "Let's get the hell out of here," I say.

I take one last glance around the family home in case it doesn't survive. "Goodbye, beloved home and all your memories." Michael snatches up the backpack and puts it on. We go out the front door and *oh my god* it's an apocalyptic hellscape out here. The electric outage must extend for miles as it's pure darkness along the roads and the sun hasn't yet begun to rise. Carried by the squall, freezing snow and ocean spray pelt us. Flood water forms what looks like a black river rushing below the house and along the street in front of us. Impossible to guess how deep it might be.

Michael holds tight to the rail on one side and me on the other. We work our way down the stairs to the top of the pool. More water flies toward us with each new wave that hits the seawall.

"Wait here!" he shouts. "I wanna see how deep it is."

I wrap my arms around the rail while he steps down into the water. When he glances back at me, I can tell from his face how bitter cold it must be. He continues to the bottom, where the water comes up to his waist. He reaches out to me. "Take my hand!"

I follow Michael, aiming to grab his hand, again reminded of Rose in *Titanic*, who dove under the frigid water without complaint to save her true love, wearing nothing more than a thin negligee. I doubt I'm capable of her level of heroism, but I'm doing my best not to scream and run back into the house. It feels like knives are stabbing all the parts of me that are underwater. I struggle to divert my brain by picturing Michael on top of me last night.

A demon wave crashes behind us, breeching the sea wall before I can reach him. It hits me with the force of river rapids, knocking me over, dragging me backwards under the water. I'm fully submerged, twisted around, and I can't tell which way is up. Mom must want me with her; she can't bear to face the ocean depths without me.

35

SEAT WARMERS

The thing I know is that I don't want to die. Not while my lips still tingle with the memory of Michael's kisses last night. Not while freedom from the cave that's enclosed me for years lies within reach. Not while I still have a mural to complete.

My lungs are close to bursting when I feel the pavement beneath my feet and I vault upward. I'm able to stand, head and torso above the water, sucking in air. I hear Michael calling my name but his voice sounds distant, almost like in a dream. The house looms in front of me; I'm facing the wrong direction. When I spin back around, Michael appears beside me and grasps my arm. Holding onto each other, we push our way through the lake that's formed, toward higher ground across the street.

We emerge from the water into the snow, which deepens as we head toward our cars. Before long, our legs are sinking up to our knees with each step, while the snow clings to our drenched clothing and slows us down with its weight.

"Just a little farther to the car." Michael's words sound slurred, which might be a symptom of hypothermia. Our movements have slowed, our breathing is labored, our teeth chatter. His face when he looks back is pale, his lips blue. I imagine I must look the same. My skin feels like ice and his must too.

"We can do this." My voice comes out like a whisper. We struggle to keep holding hands, both of us in soaked gloves stiff from freezing. I can't feel my fingers anymore. But when we turn onto the street where we parked the cars, relief washes over me. I was holding onto an irrational fear they were buried under the snow, or pulled out to sea by an errant wave, or tossed across town by the hurricane winds.

Minutes feel like an hour before we reach the SUV and climb into it. With the push of a button, the engine comes to life, but neither of us can operate the temperature controls wearing our unbending gloves. We help each other remove them, exposing damp white fingers, prickling with approaching frostbite.

"We've got seat warmers," Michael mumbles with frozen lips. He flips them on while I turn knobs to blast hot air at us.

I've no idea how long it will take to warm us back up and dry our clothes. I hope he has a full tank of gas.

36

MR. IMPERFECT

After stripping down to our underwear and verifying the extra outfits in the backpack are soaked through, we lay sprawled in our seats with the heat blasting us and our clothing. We watch the weather change in between dozing. The snowflakes lessen until they disappear; the strength of the wind diminishes from a constant howl to occasional gusts. The clouds break, revealing the rosy hue of the rising sun.

An hour later a snow plow turns onto the street. I feel my clothes. "Close enough." Though they're still somewhat damp, I choose to put on my shirt and pants rather than flash the plow driver.

Michael does the same. "I'm hungry. Where should we go?"

"Bermuda."

He nods and starts the engine.

"What about the roads?" I say. "I doubt they're all cleared."

"I could drive this baby through the Himalayas."

I like his confidence. "I need coffee."

"Starbucks? Dunkin'?"

"I doubt they're open. Let's go to the high school."

"They run a coffee shop? Has school funding come down to that?"

"It's our local warming shelter."

"Just so long as I don't have to sit through Mr. Franklin's chemistry class again."

"Somebody have some unresolved teen trauma?"

"Anyone who says they don't is lying."

I ponder this as he puts the car in low gear and we make our way. The local roads seem to have been plowed within the last couple of hours. Like Michael said, the SUV has no trouble delivering us to our destination. With my gaze sweeping the nearly full parking lot, I say, "Clearly some people were paying more attention to the weather forecast than we were."

"We had far more pressing matters on our minds last night." He gives me a lecherous look.

The gym is crowded inside, especially around the outer edges where space heaters line the walls. A man wearing a beanie and fingerless gloves and a woman with dark red hair down to her waist greet new arrivals at a table at the entrance. The woman, whose name tag says "Rai," takes our phone numbers and directs us to where we can find blankets.

"I don't suppose you have dry sweats we can change into?"

"You didn't bring a change of clothes?"

"They got submerged about the same time we did."

"Sorry. Take as many blankets as you need. The evacuation order should be over in a few hours."

We scan the gym for a place to sit near a space heater. After we have been wandering for several minutes, Michael nudges me. "Over there."

An elderly couple has risen and is gathering their belongings. We hurry to their location. "Hello," I say sweetly. "I don't suppose you're leaving?"

"You're in luck, we're going to our daughter's house in Milton."

This makes me wish *my* daughter had a house in Milton.

"I'll snag us some coffee," Michael says as soon as they've gone.

Meanwhile I peel off my jacket, wrap a warm blanket round my shoulders, and sit on the folding chair with my legs splayed in front of the heater. Moments later, Michael arrives back juggling our two cups of coffee and a paper plate holding four donuts.

"My hero," I say, grabbing one.

"I thought you didn't like donuts."

"Where on earth did you get that idea?"

"Wishful thinking?"

We savor our cheap brewed coffee and Sara Lee powdered donuts like they're Sunday brunch at the Ritz. "Thank you," I say. "If not for you, I'd be sitting on Mom's chair at the bottom of the ocean right now."

"We make a good team." He licks white powder from his upper lip. "I particularly liked our collaboration last night."

"Do you have plans for today?"

He glances around the gym. "We could help those kids build a fort out of the blankets."

"I mean work."

"Nothing I can't postpone. Not a good day to drive anywhere."

"I thought you could get through the Himalayas."

"The Himalayas, yes. Our local roads, no. Anyway, I'm not going to leave you like this. Let's hang out here awhile, then we'll check your place."

"I think the worst is over."

"Well if it's uninhabitable, there's always my humble apartment."

We make light conversation for the next hour. Everything that's happened since I met Michael bears an air of unreality. I look forward to our getting to spend a peaceful few hours in each other's company, doing nothing more exciting than sipping tea beside a toasty fire, staring out my back windows at a tranquil sea.

Occasionally he holds me in his gaze, creating a connection between us like we're wrapped in our own private, toasty-warm cocoon, hidden from everyone else in the gym. It's this sensation, this realization of what we could be to each other, that sparks hope of a possible future with him... a future in which he never needs to know how I fudged my marital status. The more I consider it, the more I convince myself I could fly home, start divorce proceedings, and fly back without Michael ever being the wiser.

These are my musings when Anthony walks into the gym and my jaw hits the floor. *Anthony...* how on earth? He's supposed to be in Newark right now. Did they divert his flight back to Boston? Or he switched airlines? Probably was on the last friggin' flight to make it into Logan. And how did he end up here at the gym rather than struggling to get to Mom's house? Most importantly, why am I asking myself all these distracting questions when nothing else matters except he's here and I have mere seconds to figure out what the fuck to do?

"You okay?" Michael is staring at my face, which no doubt has *disaster* plastered all over it.

"I'm fine. I just need to find the bathroom." I spring to my feet and set off toward the more crowded side of the gym where Anthony might not see me.

"It's the other way," Michael says.

Shit. That way leads to the entrance where Anthony now hovers by the registration table.

"I'm not in a rush," I say. "Need to walk a little first."

Possible plans race through my head. I could circle around, avoiding Anthony, and flee out the door, ditching both of them. Anthony would figure I wasn't there, while Michael would understandably be upset that I left without saying anything. I could text him in five minutes, tell him someone needed help outside. I could hide behind a tree while Anthony drives away and then return to Michael inside.

But when I glance back at Michael, I discover to my horror that Anthony is directly approaching him. How could that be? He must've glimpsed us together, it's the only explanation. If he talks to him... oh god... why, oh why didn't I tell Michael the truth? It will be a thousand times worse coming from my husband.

"Do you know where Viola went?" Anthony says to Michael in an accusing voice.

Michael is understandably baffled. "Um, who are you?"

I jump out from where I've hidden behind a post. "Anthony," I call out before he can say, *her husband.* I step forward and give him the sort of hug reserved for casual friends. "What a surprise! Can I talk to you?" I throw Michael a look meant to convey, *give me a minute to get rid of this guy.*

Anthony doesn't budge, however. "Who's your friend?" he says.

"I'm Michael Duskin." He holds out his hand to shake but Anthony ignores it.

"How long have you known my wife?" Anthony says.

At this moment I pray that a transporter beam finds me and teleports me away to the planet Vulcan.

"Wife?" Michael says.

Anthony shifts his gaze back to me. "Viola."

I wilt under the attention of both of them. "Is this your ex-husband?" Michael says.

"Excuse me." Anthony's tone is frigid. "We're not divorced."

"Just separated?"

"Aside from the nearly two months she's been at her mother's house, no, not at all."

If their two sets of eyes could project laser beams, I'd be dead right now. "Is this true?" Michael says.

I sense that more lies will only deepen the grave I've dug for myself. "Yes."

Michael turns away from me in stony silence and stalks toward the exit. "Wait," I say.

"Viola, stay here," Anthony commands.

I ignore my husband and chase after Michael. "You don't understand." I trot up beside him. "You need to know... I really care about you."

"Is that why you lied about being divorced?"

"I was just exploring. I wanted to see who was out there in the dating world. I didn't think—"

"Exploring?" He blanches.

"I don't mean with you."

"The roses at your house? He sent them?"

No more lies. "Yes."

"You just wanted to fool around. Have some fun at your husband's expense? I never would've thought..." He shakes his head in disgust.

"Oh come on." Heat rises inside me. "Men do it all the time."

"Really? So you're the expert?"

"I've read articles." I'm painfully aware how lame I sound, but can't stop myself. "Lots of guys lie about their marital status on dating apps."

"Well, I didn't lie. I hate lying."

"But you're not exactly Mr. Perfect when it comes to relationships." *Just keep shoveling,* my bad angel whispers. The look on his face shows I've jabbed him where he's most sensitive.

"Have a nice life, Viola." He pushes the exit door open before pausing. "He won't hurt you, will he?"

"Not in any way that requires a visit to the emergency room." Life with Anthony is like getting poked every day by tiny sharp needles that sting without drawing blood. Even after years, the wounds don't kill you but sometimes you wish they would. I suppose Michael figures any other damage my husband might do is beyond his understanding or ability to prevent, because he says nothing further before disappearing outside, letting the door bang shut behind him, while I watch in helpless indecision wondering why I'm my own worst enemy.

The impulse to run after him shoots through me, but I squash it. Michael's self-righteous anger has pissed me off. Maybe I was wrong about him. Maybe all men are narcissistic assholes. I wonder if hypnosis could turn me into a lesbian.

Against my better judgment, I cross the gym back to where I left Anthony. "I suppose you want an explanation."

"Later." His voice has a wounded quality. "I want to go."

"Why did you come?"

"Because you're my wife and I love you and I want you to come home with me."

"What if I tell you I don't want to come home?"

His eyes fill with tears. I've only seen him cry once before, when his mother died.

"Don't do this." His voice chokes up.

I fight back the inner desire to comfort him, reminding myself what started all this—Mom's confession regarding their affair. It's not too late, I could still run after Michael. I could tell him I've decided to leave my husband and plead with him to forgive me and take me back.

"Don't leave me, Vi," Anthony says. "Do all our years of marriage mean nothing?" He presses his hands over his face.

The problem is they mean too much. I tell him to sit down and hand him my blanket to wipe his cheeks. "I'll get you coffee." It gives me an excuse to get away from him.

At the coffee station, there's already a little book nook where some people have donated reading material. I snatch a history book about the American revolution and bring it back to Anthony along with his drink and donut. "I'm going to get the car," I say, thinking I'd far rather trudge through a frozen wasteland than have to wait beside him here. "I'll come back for you."

"Where is it?"

"Near the house. A couple miles."

"You can't walk in this weather."

"Oh yes I can." He still doesn't get the deep significance of where you are born, and how it becomes tightly wound up with who you are and what you're capable of achieving.

He doesn't argue any further. The one thing he does understand is that I've always taken care of him and done the things I said I would do. This is why he can't bear for me to leave the marriage, even if I have taken a lover.

37

___

TRAIN TO NOWHERE

I half-hope to find Michael still in his Lexus in the parking lot hesitating to leave, wondering if somehow our relationship can be salvaged. But he's gone, truly gone, and he made it clear I'll never hear from him again.

The nor'easter has blown out as quickly as it blew in. Clouds still mostly block the sun but the snow has ended and the breeze has lightened. However, it feels as if the temperature has dipped to single digits.

The main road is fully plowed as far as I can see, but the sidewalks haven't been cleared. I have no choice but to walk on the road. There isn't much traffic and anyway I really don't care who has to drive around me even if that means blocking cars in the other direction. I head away from the school in the direction of home but I'm not thinking about home.

Why is it so hard for me to find happiness? A tragic flaw of mine must've caused me to put up with a manner of living that wasn't to my liking and this is the result. At any moment during our marriage, I could simply have said, no, Anthony, I don't like how you treat me and I am leaving. He's not a violent man; he never would have stopped me. I still don't understand why I didn't do that.

Michael's face flashes in my mind. I remember the firm touch of his hands from last night. The gentleness of his lips. The way he looked at me steadily while we made love, conveying pleasure and reassurance.

Tears sting my eyes. I shake the remembrance out of me. I no longer own these memories. It's not how Michael feels about me anymore.

I pick my way along the bumpy mixture of salt, sand, and crunched-up icy snow along the side of the road. It's slow-going but I don't care, even when cars go by and spray me with the dirty mixture. My thoughts are a million miles away.

Instinct draws me toward home and the sea. It always has, ever since I was a child growing up in this town, finding my own way around on foot the way kids did in those days. We'd go out in the morning and come back at dusk, with no phones allowing our parents to keep track of us. Things were so different then.

I picture Mom's chair as we pushed it over the railing into the ocean. It needed to be done, I made her a promise, but now, in my hour of need, I yearn to hear her voice again. I wonder if the chair is really gone or if I'll find it on the beach at low tide, broken and abandoned by the sea that should've claimed her. I can't really bear the thought of it, so much like the fear I had of finding Mom herself like that, at the bottom of our stairs, broken and forsaken.

If the waves did take her, well that might be a sign I did the right thing for once. Mom, why did you have to be so complicated? I loved you since the first day I can remember looking up into your animated face, your warm brown eyes. You were the bright shining star of our family and all of us adored you. But I also hated you. Hated the influence you wielded over me.

Hated the way you sized me up as being passive and agreeable. The way you insisted I would never change. More than anything, I hate that you sampled my husband before granting him your approval to court me.

I hate that now, at age sixty-three, I'm still doing everything in my power to avoid conflict. Though you threw him my way, I didn't have to pick Anthony. Like always, I chose the path of least resistance. He was strong-willed and determined to make me his own; how was I to resist that? I didn't understand the qualities that drew him to me were the very ones I most wanted to change. Now I snort at the irony of our being at cross-purposes. Me thinking I needed to be more assertive, with him constantly pushing back on that.

He gave the appearance of deferring to me, at least in the beginning. Later, he would tell me he was henpecked. This came whenever I asked for help. It made me question myself, naturally. Was I ordering him about? Was I being a bully? Was I being unfair, asking too much of him?

I should've paid attention to what he did, not what he said. Because now looking back, it's clear as day. We lived where he wanted to live, we ate the foods he wanted to eat, we traveled where he wanted to travel, we had no pets because he didn't like them, even the trees surrounding our house were all of a single type because he liked uniformity. In the end, I always submitted to his choices because, as you knew so well, I am the Great Conflict Avoider.

I pay no attention to where I'm going, immersed in my thoughts. I don't see or hear anything outside of my head until abruptly I notice a dinging sound and red flashing lights. I'm still not sure if it's part of my imagination or outside in the real world surrounding me. My brain is a fog.

The thunderous blast of a horn shocks me out of my stupor. My vision sharpens and I see that I've reached the train crossing. I'm standing by the tracks while a train speeds toward me.

I have only an instant to decide, and my first thought is that if I take just one leap forward, I'll surely be in the path of that train, and after it hits me, I will never again have to think about Mom or Anthony or most of all Michael whose departure has shattered my heart.

38

SHE'S REALLY GONE

Jumping backwards, I land on my ass, gasping for breath as the massive train screams past me, its furious horn still blaring. My body shakes violently as I drag myself up and run across the tracks in its wake. Thankfully, the road is empty and no one but the train conductor and perhaps a few passengers could've observed my brush with death.

It's a revelation that I feel grateful to be alive. For an instant I believed I would be better off dead, but now I realize how wrong that thought was. No matter what happens next, I choose life.

My head is almost clear as I walk the rest of the way home. The flooding in the street has receded, but not completely. What remains is mostly frozen. I make my way across the ice to the front steps and into the house. The power is still off, but the good news is there's little damage to the inside, perhaps only the crack through one of the windows. I go out back to the deck and look out at the rocky beach, where it's nearly low tide now. Relief floods me to see Mom's chair is gone. The ocean took her, and kept her. Now may her chair be home to many small creatures.

When I return inside the house, I glance at the mural, almost expecting her chair to have appeared in the painting, but I guess I'll need to do that myself. "Mom?" I say to the empty spot in the family room where the chair used to be. She doesn't answer.

I let her go, as I should've years ago. I suppose I've finally grown up. I'll have to make my own decisions from now on. Mom will always be in my heart but not my head.

I return to the car outside. My husband is waiting to be picked up.

39

FLIGHT

I got us on a flight out of Boston in the evening. We couldn't stay in Mom's house without heat and electricity, but more importantly, the house has become my private thing and I don't want to share it with Anthony. God knows what he would think of the mural and even worse, the broken bed.

There's no one in the middle seat between us on the flight. In the old days, I would've sat there to be near him, so that we could let our arms and legs brush against each other while we talked. Now we leave the seat empty and keep our distance. Because of this, it almost makes me laugh when Anthony says, "I feel like you've become really distant and I don't know why."

"The fact that you don't know why is the reason we're so distant," I say. This is true. It's his utter lack of awareness regarding our problems that keeps us from being able to solve them.

"I don't know what that means." His words illustrate my point. He reaches across the chasm to take my hand but I pull it away.

"Are you in love with that guy?" he says.

I shake my head. "There's nothing between me and any man." I mean that to include Anthony.

He gives me a sideways glance. "Tell me what I can do to save this marriage."

My first thought is that it's way beyond saving. If Michael were still in the picture, that would be true. But with him gone... I'm not sure. Divorce is hard. It means living alone and getting by on less money. If Anthony is truly motivated to change, maybe I should stay.

"There have to be conditions," I say.

"Go ahead."

"Joint counseling."

He narrows his eyes. A moment later, he nods. "All right."

This surprises me. From time to time throughout our marriage, I've suggested we might benefit from a little counseling, but he's always been strongly against it. Maybe I've been wrong about him. Maybe the man can actually change.

"You need to do more chores. I've always done them, even when we were both working full time. Now it's your turn."

"I know you've had to handle most of the housework. I can do more."

"There's other jobs. Taking out the trash, hiring workers, financial management—we need to share all of them."

"My book's almost done. I'll start helping you a lot more soon."

I probably should, but I don't pick on his use of *helping you*, which always puts the responsibility of household management on my shoulders and makes it appear how generous he's being in taking on a bit of what he considers to be my load of work. At least he is making concessions. He's never done that before.

"I'll need to go back east again soon. There's still a lot for me to do to get the house ready to sell. I don't want to hear any complaints. If I can get a good price, we both benefit."

"All right." His voice sounds cranky. "Do what you need to do."

"Be glad I'm not asking you to help with that." I'm not asking for help because I don't want him to enter the house or see the mural. I'm going to paint over it; that part of my life is over. But I don't want him to know it was ever even there.

This time when he reaches for my hand I don't draw away. "I'm sure we can make things work between us again," he says. "I love you. I've always loved you."

He's the father of our child. I've taken care of him most of my life. I suppose that must be love.

40

ONE UPMANSHIP

I'm not ready to share a bed with Anthony again. When we get home, I tell him I'll be sleeping in the guest bedroom.

"Is that really necessary?" he asks.

"I need time. Let's see how the counseling goes."

A few days later, after taking advantage of a cancellation, we see Marcia, our new couples therapist.

"Great to meet you guys," she says. "Sit where you like."

I watch Anthony start at the sight of a large gray male cat that appears from behind the couch.

"Anthony's allergic," I say through force of habit. *I need to stop handling everything for him.*

"Sorry, he's here for a few days while my house is being fumigated. He won't get in our way." She adds, "Will you, Buster?" in a high-pitched voice.

"It's all right." Anthony sits on the chair next to the couch and immediately Buster springs into his lap. Normally if this happened my husband would jump up to push the cat off but he doesn't. I see what he's doing, trying to win over the therapist by pretending he's someone who likes animals.

I sit on the couch on the side opposite Anthony's chair, while Marcia is at the desk with a notepad and pen in front of her. Glancing around, I count five tissue boxes within easy reach. How much misery will need to be dragged out of us before we empty them, I wonder.

Introducing herself and her qualifications, Marcia uses a gentle tone like she's talking to children. I suppose people who can't get along after many years together have not reached the maturity of adults.

Marcia warms us up with a set of basic questions about our relationship. How many years have we been married? Do we both work outside the home? Doing what? Full-time or part-time? Inside the home, what is the division of labor? What responsibilities do we each have? How many kids and how old? Do we have grandchildren?

Though Anthony hates divulging personal matters to strangers, he responds as cheerfully and unreservedly as if he were discussing probing comments following one of his lectures. He has come prepared to put on a show for her.

"I'd like to delve a little deeper now. Would one of you like to talk about what brought you here today?" Marcia asks.

Anthony takes advantage of my hesitation to interject. "I would."

Seeing no objection from me, she prods him to go ahead.

"Viola has been having an affair."

I feel like he just broadsided me. "Is that what you think?"

"Well it's true, isn't it?" he says.

"You slept with my mother."

I feel a wave of satisfaction watching the color drain from his face. I'm deeply curious to find out if he'll acknowledge what happened. The silence extends for one minute, and then another.

"I have cancer," he says. "I flew to Massachusetts to tell you that."

Oh my god, it's like a game of one-upmanship that's moving too fast. There's only one way to beat him. "I swallowed strychnine and I'll be dead before this session is over."

"What is wrong with you?" Anthony looks disgusted.

"I'm going to assume that was a joke," Marcia says and I don't contradict her.

"Mine wasn't," Anthony says.

He's serious, I realize. He has cancer. Heat flushes through me. *How dare he get cancer? How dare he fling his diagnosis at me, just when I've finally found the courage to speak my mind?*

"Okay," says Marcia. "You guys don't mess around. There's a lot to parse here. Let's backup and take this one at a time. Viola, do you want to respond to Anthony saying you're having an affair?"

"Sure. I'm not having an affair. I did sleep with another man one time while I was away, but I won't be seeing him again."

Anthony's face has lowered over his lap and his hands are clenched into fists. Buster the cat is unfazed.

"Anthony?" Marcia says gently.

"You wanted to punish me, is that it?" he says. "Is that why you did it?"

A tornado of answers swirls inside my head. *I did it because you slept with Mom and no one told me. Because the Internet was invented since the last time you said you were sorry for anything. Because I ran out of give but you're still taking.*

But I realize this is the real answer: "It wasn't about you. It may have started that way. In the end, I didn't think about you at all. I did it for me."

Anthony snatches a tissue from the box beside him and presses it to his eyes. "Do you love him?"

I shrug. "I don't know." My heart beats faster but it doesn't matter. Michael is gone.

"How does this make you feel?" Marcia asks Anthony.

"Devastated." He blows his nose loudly.

"I'd like to hear what you have to say about having sex with my mother."

"How long have you known?" he asks.

"Irrelevant."

"It happened once, months before I met you. It meant nothing to either of us. I'm sure you had sex before you met me."

"Not with your father."

"I didn't tell you because I fell in love with you quickly and wanted to marry you. I was afraid if you knew, you'd never say yes. I kept it secret for your sake, Viola."

"Because you thought you were god's gift to the world and I would be blessed to have you?"

Marcia intervenes. "Sarcasm is unproductive, Viola."

I swallow back a retort. "So you're not planning to apologize?"

"I can't be sorry for an action that led to your becoming my wife."

"Even if I was denied the chance to make an informed decision based on full disclosure of the facts?"

"Nothing can be gained by further discussion of this," Anthony says.

We've reached an impasse. I'm wondering when we get to the counseling that's going to save our marriage. We simmer silently, avoiding each other's gaze, while Buster insists on purring even though Anthony refuses to pet him. I want to tell the cat, *don't bother, sweet talking will get you nowhere with this man.*

"We're nearly out of time, but you did bring up cancer, Anthony," Marcia says.

"Nice that one of you remembered."

I notice she doesn't scold *him* for sarcasm.

"I'm sorry to hear you have cancer." I emphasize "sorry," almost spitting it out, failing to suppress my resentment over

Anthony's refusal ever to produce that word even with pliers down his throat. "What kind of cancer is it?"

"Prostate. I'll probably need surgery." He turns to me and reaches out his hand. In a moment of weakness, I take it.

"Cancer or not, I can't live without you, Vi. You're everything to me. You always have been."

My hand burns in his grasp. *Don't feel sorry for him, don't feel sorry for him, don't feel sorry for him,* I repeat inside my head like a mantra.

41

DEPENDS

Anthony guilts me into accompanying him to his urology appointment the following day. We've hardly spoken since our appointment with the therapist, but he tries to make small talk during the car ride.

"It must feel good to be back in California. Look at this day," he says.

The weather could not be more perfect—seventy degrees in late February, not a cloud in the sky. The hills are green thanks to copious amounts of rain in December. Flowers are blooming.

"I prefer Massachusetts," I say. "I grew up with seasons. That expectation of change, it gets in your blood."

"I grew up with seasons too. But I wouldn't give up this climate for anything."

"I know you feel that way." I never felt that way. I didn't want to leave Massachusetts, despite Stanford offering more money.

"You seemed happy to live here before," he says. "What changed?"

"I did. I've changed."

"I haven't. What caused you to change?" There's a heaviness to his tone expressing his deep dissatisfaction.

"You make it sound like a bad thing."

"Isn't it? We used to feel the same way about things."

Under his influence, I used to think like him. It was never the other way around. "Change is growth. Learning. Maturity. The opposite of change is stagnation."

"The opposite of change is loyalty. Steadfastness. Faithfulness."

"And control," I say.

The conversation dwindles. What is there to say when you see the world through different lenses?

After checking in at the doctor's office, we settle in for what could be a long time judging by the number of patients waiting. Anthony who has brought his laptop finds a quiet corner with a straight-backed chair to work on his book.

I take a cushiony spot by the window, with sunshine streaming in to warm my back. I lean back and rest my head against the chair, feeling drowsy. Not far from the reception desk, I can't help hearing the conversation of a couple waiting in line for check-in.

"Have we come to the right place for my penis reduction surgery?" the man says.

I stifle a laugh and glance over at him and his wife or partner, who are holding hands facing away from me. In the haze of the filtered sunlight, he reminds me of Michael. He even sounds like Michael.

"Not quite, darling," says the woman, who looks like me as far as I can tell from the back of her, and speaks in my voice. I swear, if it wasn't impossible, I'd say she *was* me. "I think they call it prostate removal," she adds.

"They can call it what they like. You sure you won't mind?"

"I don't think we'll miss it, love."

"What about the recovery time? Can you wait a full year if it takes that long? You won't run off with the pool boy?"

"We don't have a pool."

"Good reason not to get one. Do we have milk delivery?"

"Discontinued in 1935."

"What about the mailman? He's rather handsome, isn't he?"

"He won't come into the house. Afraid we might have dogs."

"So I have nothing to worry about?"

"I can be patient."

"I bought my new Depends. I got the purple ones."

"Lovely. When will you model them for me?"

"I could put on a show for you tonight."

"Can we stop at the bank on the way home? I need to get some hundreds to slip in your waistband."

"Hundreds, eh? Am I worth that much? I'm just a beginner."

"You've always been a good dancer."

"Should we invite your friends? I mean, if the going rate for a strip tease is in the hundreds, this could help pay our medical bills."

"I might be jealous."

"You're the only one for me, baby." He puts his arm around her and draws her close. His voice goes quiet, his tone vulnerable. "What if I can't get it up ever again?"

"The penis is overrated."

"A man would never say that."

"Then be happy I'm a woman who values your heart and mind over your other parts."

"I'm so lucky to have you."

"Besides, there are always vibrators."

Reception calls them to the counter and I close my eyes, feeling a nap coming on. A noise makes me open them again a few minutes later, just as the couple turns away from reception and sets off to find seats. Funny. They don't look anything like Michael or me.

I stare down the row at Anthony, his forehead furrowed as he concentrates on his book. He's like a stranger to me.

42

YOUR BIG FAT SELF

"When are you coming back here?" Jackie asks.

It's our first phone call since I returned to California. She's tried reaching me several times, but I haven't answered till now. I was afraid talking to her would remind me of the freedom and happiness I experienced in Windset, which I imagine I'll never get back. But because it's wrong to ignore my friend, I made myself pick up today.

"What do you mean, when am I coming back? Didn't you hear what I just said?" I spent the last ten minutes filling her in on Anthony's cancer and his upcoming surgery to remove his prostate. "What kind of monster leaves their spouse of almost forty years after they get a cancer diagnosis?"

"I don't think you're looking at it the right way."

"It's hard to imagine anything worse than that. I suppose it's one step up from murder. My daughter would disown me, I'm sure of it. And I really was ready to leave him, you know. I was checking local listings for divorce attorneys. But the man can barely take care of himself when he's healthy —what's going to happen during his year of recovering after the surgery? What's going to happen if the cancer has spread and it's not just one surgery but a series of them, and radiation, and chemo—treatments that could last for years?"

"So this is a death sentence for both of you?"

"He's not going to die from this."

"But he'll be dealing with medical treatments, and you'll give up a minimum of a year of your life providing support. Is that it?"

"Pretty much."

"Haven't you given enough?"

"Yeah, but—"

"Do you deserve to be happy?"

"Sure, but—"

"No buts. Do you deserve to be happy?"

"I guess."

"Is Anthony's happiness more important than yours?"

"No!"

"Are you sure? That's what your actions say. What would you do if you put your happiness first?"

"I don't know."

"Did you ever watch *Frozen*?"

"Yeah, yeah, I know, *let it go*."

"I'm not saying what you think. Elsa has an incredible talent. But all her life, her parents and everyone around her have told her to suppress it. To act like she's ordinary.

"And then one day she accidentally releases her power for all to see. And she runs away feeling like a pariah—until she has a transformation. That's when she sings 'Let It Go.' She's already let the secret out, but the difference is, now she gives herself permission. She revels in her power. She's special and why must she hide it?

"Our generation was taught to hide our greatness. To be the shadow behind a man. Our mothers certainly did that. Why stay with any man who wants to keep you that way? *Let it go* means *release my power.* Be your big, fat, wondrous, gorgeous, talented self."

"Fat?"

"Stop it. You know what I mean."

And like that, I have a revelation. At this point in my life, it's no longer about Anthony or Mom, or Anthony and Mom. It's about me, and what kind of life I want for myself moving forward.

I feel like zapping a few things.

43

THE NEW ME, THE OLD HIM

I observe Anthony carefully for the next week. It's fascinating to see what happens now that he feels secure. He knows the old me well. He doesn't understand the new me.

The old me would never have considered leaving him at his time of greatest need. It was absolutely impossible that I would divorce him following a cancer diagnosis. He could commit any amount of bad behavior and I would shove it under the carpet and soldier on.

The new me is paying attention. I'm making a point of observing if the changes he said he would make are going to stick.

The first to go are the counseling sessions. "There's no point in going back there," he tells me. "Did she give us any helpful advice? No."

"I'm not sure that's really the point of therapy."

The next day he asks if I called any of the contractors on the list he sent me.

"Why would I do that? You agreed we would use Lopez."

"The first guy? I told you his estimate was too high."

"But after that you said it was okay."

"I would remember that," Anthony says.

He lights the flames for his own cremation when I'm in my study and he calls me from the kitchen. "Vi, can you come down here?"

When I get there, he shows me what he describes as a sticky spot on the floor.

"Do you know what it is?" he asks like he expects me to drop on all fours and do a chemical analysis before cleaning it.

"My ticket to freedom," I say. A giddy happiness bubbles up inside me. Anthony has finally given me reason to celebrate. He has proven himself incapable of change. And now I know what to do.

I call a divorce attorney and get her started on filing for my divorce. I book my flight to Boston. I pack my suitcase. The last thing I do before taking a ride to the airport is speak to Anthony. This is because I don't wish to be around him while he brings out his full array of manipulative techniques. They no longer work on me, but they're painful to sit through and a waste of our time.

He's in his study when I enter wearing my coat. "I'm leaving now, Anthony."

He looks up, distracted. "Where are you going?"

"Home."

"You are home."

"Not anymore. We're getting a divorce."

"You can't do that. I need you. Do I have to remind you I have cancer?"

"There are resources. Figure it out. I'm done."

I head toward the front door.

"You can't leave me, Vi!" There's the dissonance of panic in his voice.

Instead of answering, I demonstrate how it is, in fact, possible for me to leave him. I take my suitcase waiting at the door and step outside where my ride awaits. The sun is shining and a soft breeze brushes my cheeks. I breathe in the scent of our neighbor's sturdy redwood and straighten my stance.

I call Max before I board my flight. Anthony may have already told her and I don't want her to face a long wait before talking to me.

Sure enough, her first words are, "Mom, what the hell are you doing?" Her voice is thick with crying.

"I hope you understand this has nothing to do with you. We both love you as much as always. This is about your father and me and our irreconcilable differences."

"He has cancer! And he can barely tie his shoes without you. I thought you loved him!"

"I did love him."

"Why are you leaving him? Is there someone else?"

"No, sweetheart. He wore me down. Living with him makes me unhappy."

"Why don't you try counseling? He said he's willing."

"He says a lot of things he doesn't mean. It's over, Max. I hope you'll come to understand the reasons."

"You're being selfish! Dad needs you now more than ever."

"I love you. I'll call you next week."

"Don't you dare hang—"

I hang up. I'm prepared to move on with my life with or without my daughter's approval. Though I wish I could've made her understand, as I fly off toward eastern skies, I feel as light as the clouds floating past my window.

44

THE MISSED SIGN

Although it reminds me of the fleeting chapter in my life when I was hopeful of a new relationship, I admire the mermaid weathervane on top of my house whenever I'm outside, especially the way it catches the light on a bright day. I had it installed shortly after returning to Windset seven months ago with the intention of settling permanently into Mom's house. Since that time, my life has changed in almost every way imaginable.

The house is in good shape now. I paid for the needed repairs and for fresh paint inside and out, with the exception of the wall with the mural of course. The bathrooms would benefit from upgrades, but I'm not in any rush. The place feels as comfortable as an old pair of boots, which suits me just fine.

I adopted a dog from the shelter. She's an Aussie shepherd mini blended with something, I'm not sure what. It doesn't matter. She is a small, fuzzy bundle of irrepressible energy. I named her Aggie after *Agnes Grey*, a book by Anne Brontë, the least celebrated of the sisters, about a journey of self-discovery by the title character. Three years old, but she still looks like a pup. Lives for retrieving balls on the beach and in the ocean. I propped steps by the bed so she can climb up and sleep beside me.

Every morning and evening we go for walks along the shore. Sometimes Poppy—a husky-shepherd mix—and her human Debbie join us. I had forgotten how friendly New Englanders are. I've never been as connected to my community as I am now. This must be one of the few places in the world where you can become instant pals with your local dry cleaner, or pharmacist, or check-out clerk. Outsiders sometimes call us blunt, but *direct* is a more accurate adjective. You know where you stand with us.

I finished the mural. A young woman, having survived the shipwreck, swims toward the surface. Pelicans swoop overhead and vibrant sea creatures populate the ocean. Mom's chair has settled at the bottom of the sea and an octopus peeks out from underneath it, because who doesn't love an octopus?

My divorce became final one week ago. It hasn't been easy, but I think it proceeded smoother than most. Anthony didn't want to invest the time or money that would've been required to contest anything, so he agreed to the reasonable terms my lawyer laid out. I told him I would be satisfied with my share as required by California law.

After a few months of silence, my daughter began speaking to me again. She's helping me plan her grandmother's celebration of life, pushed out to the end of September due to the dwindling hope we might still recover her ashes in time. I'm sure Max still wishes her father and I were together, but at least now she appears to understand how I felt in the marriage. She told me recently that Anthony is doing okay and dipping his toe into online dating. Unsurprisingly, he hasn't gotten the prostate surgery, and may never. According to Max, prostate cancer grows slowly, and therefore Anthony's doctor advised that he test often and hold off on surgery as long as the PSA in his blood—prostate specific antigen—doesn't rise. Anthony exaggerated the urgency, the complications, and the length of the recovery period when he told me about it. Do I spend restless nights dreaming of vengeance? Not at all. I'm learning to let go.

I've greeted the official demise of my marriage with mixed feelings. I celebrated with a night of drinking and dancing with Jackie, Ken, Freddie, and several newer friends at the tavern. Overall, I'm giddy with the sensation of freedom and looking forward to discovering what makes me happy when my choices aren't tempered by Anthony's disapproval. But sometimes at night I still see Michael in my dreams.

Today I'm diving into a project I put off since Mom's death because it's been too painful to look at her photos and know I'll never see her alive again. At last, having gotten past the trauma of the divorce, I'm ready to face the emotional task of going through her photo albums. Enough time has passed that I'm eager to awaken my memories of her and Dad and Keaton through the pictures she saved of us. For the first time in my life, I'm grateful for her diligence in maintaining the albums.

They have themes. Each of what Mom considered to be the important holidays—Thanksgiving, Christmas, Easter, 4th of July, and Halloween—have several albums dedicated to them. The pictures from each year are remarkably similar to those of the prior years, except for the differences as we aged. An evolving group of friends is woven throughout the background of our family narrative. In one high school photo, I spot Jackie with her shag hairstyle and mini-skirt.

In the Halloween series, Mom took all the pictures since she never wore a costume herself. Dad wore his regular clothes and put on a different rubber monster mask each year. My favorite was King Kong, though I recognize now how the giant ape story represented the male fantasy of a woman falling in love with her abusive lover.

For some reason, Keaton was always a ghost. Every

Halloween he wore the same white sheet with eyeholes. It was a simple costume, easily repeated. Looking at his pictures, it seems obvious to me now that Keaton never felt seen, not really, not for who he really was. It's heartbreaking to look at him hiding under his sheet, waiting for the moment that never comes to throw it off and show off his rainbow colors.

I was always disappointed at Halloween because I dreamt of being a princess or a ballerina or a runway model, but Mom rejected what she called *girlie costumes* for me. One year I asked her how come I couldn't wear frilly dresses when she wore them all the time. She said, "It's too late for me, but you'll thank me later for putting you on the path toward true feminism." She coerced me into a series of stereotypically male costumes: car mechanic, biker dude, construction worker, mad scientist. If only the feminism had come naturally from inside me, instead of being forced by Mom, which made me want to reject it.

After the holidays, I jump to the set of albums filled with photos representing all the "first" activities performed by Keaton and me. First bites of food, first steps, and first words—with "Mama" neatly printed next to both our pictures, making me question whether the whole project was more a reflection of revised history than truth. First day at nursery school, as we called it then, followed by first day in every grade until we graduated. The photos bring back a variety of memories, both joyous and sad. When I'm nearly at the end of all the "firsts," my emotions are overwhelming me and I'm ready to set the rest of this project aside for another few weeks.

But on turning to the last page, I arrive at an event I've thought little about over the years, despite that it made a huge impression at the time. My first car purchase at the age of twenty-one. I recall desperately wanting the bright red bug and instead getting the puke green Dodge. Somehow that's a stronger memory than my almost getting killed by the homicidal, disgruntled ex-employee. Mom kept two pictures recording the incident: one that she took with her Polaroid, and the other a black and white that was printed in the newspaper.

Our names are captioned under the news photo. The name Michael catches my eye, and then I see his last name: Duskin. Michael Duskin. I stare in disbelief. *Michael Duskin*—the man I loved and lost during my brief foray into online dating. I peer more closely at the photo. Oh my god, it really is him. I also check the photo Mom took of us that day, where I can see his features more clearly and in color. It really is Michael.

Goosebumps tickle the back of my neck. I lower the scrap-book and stare out at the sky, remembering present-day Michael telling me he started out in the car business before some crazy incident made him switch to construction. I recall being attracted to the nice young man at the used car lot. If he'd asked me out, I would've said yes.

This is a sign if I ever saw one. How dense I was to have missed it. I mean, the two of us nearly killed—in each other's arms. But I was distracted by my pathetic little rebellion against Mom's car choice and oblivious to the life and death drama playing out right in front of me.

45

TARGET

I'm walking toward the entrance of our local Target when I spot the car. A silver Mercedes sedan with a slight dent on the back right side. Most importantly, it has a Red Sox decal in the form of a pair of red socks.

I creep up next to it, probably looking like a car thief casing my next job. Actually I just want to peer inside to see if I can find any identifying information. There's a red scarf on the passenger seat, and several reusable shopping bags from Trader Joe's in the back. Though he's almost certainly a crook and a scam artist, at least he's doing his part to rid the world of plastic.

Should I call the police? Last month Detective Dempsey informed me the case was still open though they had zero leads. But it might take too long if I dial the number for the station.

I call 9-1-1.

"What is your emergency?"

It's hard explaining this without sounding like I'm missing a few marbles. "My mother was stolen... I mean her ashes... Detective Dempsey is handling the case... there's a car here with a Red Sox decal... it belongs to some scammer who was dating her... you know, before she died—"

"We're sending an officer over. Wait outside the store till the officer arrives. Do not attempt to approach the suspect."

"Thanks." I hang up before asking if I should keep the line open. Because naturally I have no intention of following her instructions.

He must be inside Target. No other businesses are in the vicinity, so why else would he park there? But there's no point in my searching the whole store. It's way too large, and he could easily head back to his car while I'm trying to find him in the men's baseball team clothing section. Instead, I enter the store and wait for him by the exit, hoping I recognize him from the dim memory I have of Mom's visitation.

A large display of seasonal items lures shoppers near the front. The theme is weddings, probably because the weather is warm and we're between holidays. Marriages are probably my least favorite topic at the moment, given the recent collapse of my own, not to mention Max having broken up with her boyfriend, but this is a minor consideration compared to the possibility of nailing Mom's larcenous date. I pour over the wedding planner magazines, the Hallmark cards, and the party favors for the budget-minded.

Ten minutes later, the cops are still not here and I'm panicking that I must've missed the perpetrator after getting caught up reading about a spectacular wedding in Vermont during my favorite time of the year—fall, of course.

Then suddenly I recognize my quarry, and to my surprise, he's empty-handed. Do people come here just to browse? I've never entered the place—until now—without a list of specific items I know they carry. I had assumed I would spot the man in line at a register first, giving me time to adjust my strategy. But now, with him speed-walking toward the exit, I have no choice but to scream out, "THIEF! STOP HIM! HE'S GETTING AWAY!"

The security team—just one unassuming, bespectacled guy actually—follows my pointing finger to the culprit while I pray I have recognized the right person.

"Hey, what's going on?" the man shouts when non-threatening Security Guy takes his arm.

"Come this way please," Security Guy says.

I hurry over to them. "I saw him taking something," I say.

The man raises his arms. "Taking what? I don't have anything."

"He put it in his pocket," I say. "Some jewelry." I try to recall if Target even sells jewelry.

The man scrutinizes me. "I've seen you before."

"I believe you knew my mother," I say pointedly.

"The viewing," he says.

"I need to search you," Security Guy says.

"You stole my mother's ashes," I say.

"And they're in his pocket??" Security Guy asks. I realize I'm coming off as a demented person, which means he'll let go of the man any minute now.

"Your mother's ashes...?" the man says.

"You, or someone you know, pretended to be her husband. You took her rings and her purse too. From the hospital where she died." I burst into tears.

The man stares at me like he's trying to figure something out. "I think I know what happened. I can explain."

The squad car is just pulling up to the curb.

"Lady, what do you want me to do?" Security Guy says.

"Let him go," I say. "I'll take care of this."

The possible thief follows me outside, right up to the squad car. When the officer gets out, she greets my guy by first name. "Peter, good to see you. What's going on?"

Typical. Everybody knows everybody around here.

46

THE RED SOX

In the Target parking lot, Peter the Red Sox fan told me and the officer that his father Henry was with my mother the night she died, but he was unaware his father took anything. Peter currently lives with his dad, who suffers from dementia. He gave me the address and asked me to meet him there in an hour. The officer, convinced that Peter was no threat, headed back to the station.

An hour later, I pull up outside an adorable cottage on Summer Street in Brumewich, the town next to Windset. When I arrive, Peter is outside collecting letters from the mailbox.

"I've got the answers for you now, Viola." He beckons me through the front door. "I'm really sorry for what you've been through."

"I'm just happy the mystery is solved at last."

"Come meet my father." He ushers me into the front hallway. Though the house is old, it's meticulously clean and furnished in a charming New England style. I follow him to a sunroom in the back that looks like an add-on.

A man with fly-away white hair and untamed eyebrows is

on the couch watching a baseball game on TV. Peter turns the volume down.

"Dad, this is Rosemary's daughter. Viola, this is Henry."

Henry glances up with curious eyes. "Rosemary?"

"This is Viola."

"Hi, Henry," I say. "How are you?"

His eyes lift toward his son like he's not sure what to say.

"You're good, Dad."

Henry leans back on the sofa and looks at the game, but he doesn't react to seeing Boston score a run.

"Come with me," Peter says. I follow him out of the sunroom.

"My father talks very little these days. You know. Alzheimer's." He shrugs with resignation. "It's progressing fast. He was still able to live here alone back in January. He was even driving then. But I could tell he was having moments of confusion. I didn't move in with him till March, though. I should've come sooner."

"We all have our regrets." I'm becoming quite the philosopher.

He leads me into their living room, where Mom's box is resting on a table, with her purse beside it. I hurry over to her, overwhelmed by as much excitement as if I were greeting her in the flesh and not the ashes. I even open the box to verify it's her, and recognize the two bone fragments I saw at the funeral home. "You're back, Mom." I close the box and hold it close for a moment. "It's so good to find you again." I set her back down and look inside the purse. Mom's phone and rings are inside.

"I'm glad you reached out," Peter says. "I'm very sorry I ran away from you at the funeral home. Dad made me promise not to speak to anyone. Out of respect for her, he was still hiding their affair. That's why he didn't go himself."

I'm not certain why Peter couldn't have just pretended to be an old friend, but there's no point in making him feel worse than he does.

"I had no clue he took the ashes or the purse till today. I was trying not to violate his privacy, you know? Just now when I got back here, I searched his closet and found them hidden in a cardboard box in the back. Please know my father would never have taken these things in his normal state of mind. I'm sure he didn't know what he was doing."

He picks up a yellowed envelope and hands it to me. "I found this too. Your mother wrote it."

Henry's first name is on the envelope. It obviously didn't arrive through the post.

"From previous conversations with my dad, I understand they renewed their old acquaintance and started meeting now and then a few months before your mother passed. I'm sure they didn't get married. But he was starting to suffer from the delusion that he was her husband. After I came in March, when he talked about 'his wife,' he called her Rosemary. He was married to my mother till she died a year ago, but her name was Deirdre."

"I'm sorry."

He shrugs. "I think their marriage went sour years ago, but he hung in there for her sake. That's how he was. He clearly loved your mother. You'll see. In the letter."

I gather everything in my arms. "I plan to give her a sea burial like she wanted. Would Henry want to be there?"

He glances back at the room. "No. He barely leaves the house anymore. He wouldn't understand what was going on. Now and then, when he talks to himself, I hear him saying her name. Honestly, I think he sees her walking around. He thinks she's living here."

Funny. I thought she was living at my place. "You're a saint taking care of him," I say.

"I do my best and I'll do it for as long as I'm able."

47

OH HENRY

Oh Henry,

I've always wanted to start a letter to you like that. You remember O'Henry's story about the gifts? The girl sells her hair to buy the boy a watch chain, and he sells his watch to buy her a hairpin. When you love someone, you're well-intentioned even when you're screwing it all up. I don't suppose that's the lesson of the story, though.

I wish our story could have a happy ending. It started over gifts too, didn't it? You coming into my shop twice a year to buy presents for Deirdre's birthday and Christmas. A sad irony for her that your efforts to please her ended in your falling in love with someone else.

To our credit, we did our best to resist our feelings. It wasn't till we began getting lunch at Addison's that I knew we were in for it. No one gets me like you do, especially when it comes to our beloved Red Sox.

I cried all night yesterday after you proposed. I told you I would think about it, but I knew my answer already. I can't divorce Thomas, and you shouldn't divorce Deirdre. My Catholic training won't allow me to break my vows. Sister Priscilla would be proud of me.

Forgive me. Live your life with purpose and joy and I'll try to do the same. If we're truly soulmates, we will meet again in heaven. Know that I love you to the outfield of Fenway Park and back, but it doesn't change anything.

-R

EVERYTHING MAKES SENSE NOW, including the reason she gave up her religion in the last months before dying. Her faith kept her from divorcing Dad though she obviously loved Henry. His showing up as a widower on her doorstep must've been too much for her. I wonder if his return was what she had been waiting for before letting go of life.

The fact that she quit being Catholic at age eighty-nine for the chance to find love with Henry shows how much she must've regretted refusing him.

I don't want to be my mother.

48

THE TEXTS

Tonight there's a full moon and I consider walking down to the lighthouse and onto the breakers in the hope that Signal will show up again to give me a sign that I mustn't give up on Michael. But what if the coyote is a no-show? I refuse to take that as a sign I should give up.

Anyway, I can't imagine why Signal would waste his time shadowing a human who can't make up her own mind without the approval of a random wild animal, when he and the mate he found this winter now have a full-time job watching over a new family of pups.

It's time for me to stop waiting for anybody's permission to take action. If I send Michael a text, what's he going to do, blow up my house with a drone?

I take a picture of the photo Mom took of him and me next to the car, and another of the newspaper photo with the caption that shows Mom's and my names along with his. Then I text them along with this message: "I found these in my mother's photo album." Feeling like I've got nothing to lose at this point, I assemble a second text with two more pictures: one showing my completed mural, and another of the mermaid weathervane he gave me in its new place on my roof. I add the message, "I moved into Mom's house. My divorce was final two weeks ago."

Chances are good I'll never hear back from him, but it makes me feel better to have tried. The results of doing nothing are always nothing, whereas doing something may provoke a reaction.

The following day I stay busy working on my latest projects. Freddie the unexpected dentist who I met my first night breaking out has commissioned me to create a wall-sized African jungle scene in his waiting room. It's a joy painting it on site, watching the brightening effect its cheerful, colorful creatures have on anxious patients, particularly the children.

Later at home I continue work on a new painting Tucker the gallery owner encouraged me to do. We tried dating a few times after I returned to Windset, but when the lack of chemistry became palpable to both of us, we quickly settled into a comfortable friendship. He's currently featuring *Da Seat* at his gallery, while I paint the next entry into the "series," though I'm not sure this latest is even terribly related. Still, like Mom's chair, it has a dark theme. It's a depiction of the car crash at the used auto dealership where, if I'd only known, the more momentous occurrence was actually meeting Michael. For this reason, I'm putting the couple in the foreground with the man's arms still wrapped around the young woman after pulling her out of harm's way, and the two smashed up cars in the background with black smoke curling above them.

I see Jackie a lot too, usually over lunch, and she's been re-introducing me to other high school classmates. Who knew I had such nice and interesting friends back then? Life is good. It's much better with no partner than with a mismatched one. We are here for too short a time to sacrifice any part of it for someone you picked when you were still a child, and who you later came to realize was not your perfect match after all.

It isn't till late evening that I notice a text I missed while I was out walking Aggie. Michael has replied.

49

SAFE HARBOR

I'm afraid to read it. What if it's, *stop contacting me or I'll call the police?* Or, *does disaster just follow you everywhere?* Or worst of all, *leave me alone, I'm on my honeymoon.*

I sit and take several deep breaths before opening it. The message says *thanks for the photos,* which at least has a polite tone though its curtness makes my hopes sink. But a moment later, another text arrives. He must've had to think about this one a little more. *I'm on that trip I told you about, sailing and motoring my yawl serendipity along the inner coastal. We're arriving at safe harbor in savannah by day's end tomorrow, planning to stay a few days.*

I read the text over and over. How should I interpret it? Why no comment on my move to Mom's house or my mural or my divorce or the astonishing revelation of our first near-fatal meeting, for god's sake?

Most importantly, how could he use the pronoun "we" without clarifying the gender of his sailing companion?

He isn't making things easy for me. I spend the next hour researching harbors in Savannah where he might possibly moor his boat, before discovering Safe Harbor is an actual place and not just a comforting metaphor.

50

SERENDIPITY

Viola 2.0 doesn't need to wait for anyone's advice before taking action. Despite the many questions remaining in my mind, I book a flight to Savannah for the morning.

After a sleepless night preparing for my trip and arranging care for my dog, I arrive at the airport three hours in advance of my flight. When at last I settle into my window seat, my eyelids lower and I'm passed out till I feel the jet bump down on the tarmac in Georgia.

I don't know whether Michael will welcome my abrupt arrival. He might even be traveling with his latest love interest. But I'm doing this for myself. If I'm still alive twenty years from now, I don't want my lungs clogged with the bile of regret. And I know for certain that will happen if I don't give my relationship with Michael one last chance.

After downing a small latte from the airport Starbucks, I'm bouncing on my toes on the way to the rental car counter. Even if it doesn't work out—if I can't find him, or he never meant for me to come and tells me to go away—I'm still glad I'm doing this. Being bold and taking a risk makes me feel like I could float through the air. A new sense of pride fills me.

I've never visited this city before, but I enjoy driving through it. It's hot and humid as hell outside, but I blast the A/C, singing along to romantic hits from the seventies and eighties. Twice I get lost. Once I find myself in a magical neighborhood of cobblestone streets, historic buildings, and quaint shops. The next time I make a wrong turn, I end up pulling over by the riverside to watch ships passing, and summer unfolding on sandy beaches.

When I finally arrive at Safe Harbor, I have to drive around looking for parking. It's a big place, how will I even find him? He didn't tell me when he was scheduled to arrive. I suppose I could text him, but I need my visit to be a surprise. It's important for me to gage his unguarded reaction to my arrival. Before long, I pull into a parking space and set out toward one of several docks on foot.

He didn't mention whether he had a berth or a mooring, complicating the search for him. After walking around for a while, however, I realize there are few large sailboats docked. I'm not positive how big his boat is, but for a long trip like that with a companion, I can't imagine it's terribly small.

Eventually I discover a launch boat that picks up passengers from boats at moorings and brings them in. After several boaters disembark, I speak to the teenage boy who operates it.

"Have you brought anyone in from a boat called "Serendipity?"

He thinks for a moment before shaking his head. "Never heard of it."

"They're not from around here. They sailed down from Massachusetts."

"You sure they came in on the launch? They probably have their own dinghy."

"Oh. Where do the dinghies go?"

He gives me directions to another stretch of dock where a slew of small boats float in a crowded heap. I look through these, but most only have registration numbers. If only they were marked with the names of their owners' yachts.

Returning to a high point overlooking the dock, I settle on a bench watching the sun lower over the water, suffusing the sky with a crimson mantle. During this time, three motorboats and two dinghies putter up to the dock, but Michael is not a passenger on any of them.

When the last colors of the sunset are replaced by darkness, I force myself to stand and plod with heavy steps toward where I think I parked my car. I suppose I had unrealistic expectations of finding him here without knowing specifically where or when he was arriving.

After walking for ten minutes, I suspect I've made a wrong turn. Up ahead on the right, there's a sprawling building, brightly lit with a large parking lot, that I don't remember seeing earlier. It looks like a place where I could ask for directions. When I get closer, I see the sign—Safe Harbor Yacht Club—and hear the sounds of loud voices and music coming from inside. No one stops me from entering, not even to ask if I'm a member. A lengthy bar stretches along the side, and beyond that I glimpse a room with tables. The place is packed, the atmosphere lively, the guests friendly based on their welcoming smiles.

It feels like an oasis in the desert of my mood. I zero in on the nearest bartender and order a glass of generic red wine, *you can't start your car with it*, he assures me. I assume he means it tastes better than gasoline though it's suspiciously cheap at five dollars. I give the bartender a ten—still less than the total for a glass of wine in California or Massachusetts—and settle into my first sip, satisfied that it beats my ultra-low expectations.

The man and woman next to me are smiling. "Are you from out of town?" the woman asks. She and the man look so much alike I wonder if they're siblings. At five foot three or four, they are roughly the same height.

"Is it that obvious?" I ask.

"Your northern accent," she says.

"I'm from Massachusetts. Viola."

"Joe," the man says. "And my wife Mimi."

"Are you members here?"

"Almost twenty-five years," Joe says.

"I wonder if you can help me. I was expecting a Massachusetts boat called Serendipity to be arriving here today, but I didn't see it come in."

"Did you try calling the captain?" Mimi says.

"I want to surprise him."

"Oh how fun," she says, but at the same time her eyes flicker with unease and I get the feeling she thinks you might learn something it's better not to know when you surprise a man.

"Let me ask a few people," Joe says.

He wanders off to talk to others while Mimi peppers me with questions about the northeast. After a few minutes, he returns looking pleased with himself. "They came in a while ago. They're back there in the dining room. Go on in."

I could swear my blood pressure shoots up ten points. *He's here! Right now!* I absolutely was not expecting this. The news is more horrifying than joyful, if only because I'm scared shitless the other half of "they" is female.

Mimi picks up on my panicked expression and pats my arm. "Would you like us to come?"

"No." Presenting myself sandwiched between these two adorable munchkins would only offset the seriousness of my intent. "I need to do this myself."

"Good luck," they say in unison.

I press through the crowd toward the dining room, where the folks seated have ordered small bites to accompany their drinks. I was hoping to spot him from the doorway, leaving myself an easy retreat if he's with a woman. But the room extends past some posts and around a corner, making it impossible for me to view everyone from this vantage point.

"Can I get you a table?" a young man asks.

"No, thank you, I'm looking for someone."

"The Barker party? They're right over there." He gets ready to lead me to a long table filled with large men who look like they're related.

"Not them. Mind if I look around?"

"Sure, go ahead."

When I'm midway into the room, I spot Michael facing my direction at a table near the back wall. I nearly pee myself over the thrill of seeing him. It might be the tan, but he looks more handsome than ever. I'm frozen in place just breathing in the zen of him.

It's only when he speaks that I perceive the woman at his table, her back to me. I can't see her face but her hair is long, her figure slender. I crumple from a state of euphoria to the complete opposite in a mere second of time. I'm too late, he's found someone else. It's my own fault for waiting so long to reach out to him again.

I can't let him know I came here. Spinning sharply to flee, I collide with a waiter carrying a tray of dirty dishes. He drops the tray, dishes land on the floor, a glass shatters. When I look back at Michael, he's staring at me in disbelief. There's chaos in the room as staff rushes to clean up and make sure no one was hurt. I can barely breathe, overwhelmed by humiliation. My legs move, whisking me out of the dining room, through the crush of people in the bar, and out into the cool night air. I have to pause, leaning on a car, as a rush of dizziness threatens to topple me.

Footsteps slap the pavement behind me. "Viola," Michael says. "Are you okay?"

I refuse to be the object of his pity. Pulling myself together, I straighten my shoulders and turn to face him. "Nobody ever said I was graceful."

"You have your moments." His tone is soft, with a hint of amusement.

I let out a short laugh. I suppose he's thinking of our first meeting when I slipped on the ice.

"You came here." He sounds incredulous. "You actually came."

"Well, I had nothing better to do today. I've always wanted to see Savannah. Sorry to interrupt your date." I feel a dampness on my face. With horror, I discover it's tears.

"My date...?" Strangely, his face brightens.

"I really hope you find happiness. Oh, and have fun on the boat. I'm sure you're perfect for each other. I don't think I would've made a good sailor. I'll shut up now. Goodbye."

"Viola." He steps closer. "Wait."

I'm full on sobbing at this point. "Please just leave me alone."

"Viola, she's my friend's wife. It's just him and me on the boat. She flew down here to meet him today. He was in the bathroom just now."

I stutter my response. "Y-your f-friend's wife?"

"Yes. I'm not with her. I'm not with anyone."

"No one?" My lips twitch. A smile about to erupt. "Not even Cadence?"

He snorts. "Not even her. Though she did text me a few times."

"You didn't date her?"

"I was waiting for you."

"I was terrible to you."

"It was too soon. I should've been more understanding. You had a choice to make."

"Life or the semblance of it."

He opens his arms. When I raise my hands around his neck,

he wraps me in a tight embrace. I tip my head back and kiss him like we're long-lost lovers. He holds me close like we were always meant to be together.

THE END

Please visit margiebenedict.com to explore my other novels and sign up for my entertaining newsletter. Be the first to learn about new releases and books on sale.

DREADMARROW PREVIEW
A FANTASY FOR ALL AGES

Today, my fifth time as a russet sparrow, I felt as if I'd been flying all my life. I left caution behind, soaring over the town square, catching a beakful of rancid smoke rising from the shops and ramshackle homes. My wings flapped according to instinct and carried me toward Sorrenwood's outer edge, over rows of broken shelters. I continued across a field dotted with bent farmhands, past a thicket of trees that gave way to the swimming hole.

I flew lower to watch the three bare-chested boys who approached the water. I'd seen them before but they were younger than me and I could not remember their names. The dark one swung out on the rope and when he reached the highest point, he released with a shout and a splash. His friends followed in rapid succession, nearly landing on him. Their joy was infectious. I sailed up higher and dove down, letting myself fall until—an inch above the water's surface—I pulled up. The pale boy saw me and looked puzzled. He had probably never seen a bird play before.

I rose higher for my second dive. But as I shifted downward, a huge silhouette appeared above me... *a hawk*, its wings spread wide, a monstrous beast to sparrow-me. Shaking, I dodged left and then right and then back again, hoping to confuse it with my odd movements. I followed an erratic course and didn't realize until it was too late, that I'd crossed over the outer wall and now flew above the Cursed Wood. Gray mist seeped upwards like steam from a giant cauldron. The tips of black tangled branches reached toward me, but I knew better than to land on any of its foul trees.

The air whooshed as the hawk dove for me, and I felt a stinging sensation as it clipped off a wad of my feathers. I beat my wings in a panic, angling toward Fellstone Castle. It was a dreary, forbidding fortress but the only place I might find refuge. A shadow formed over me as the hawk prepared to dive again. My confidence shaken, I swore at myself for having so little practice flying. Whether to flap my wings or coast on the wind—I had no idea which would get me to the castle quicker. And so I flapped and coasted and flapped again, aiming to reach the nearest tower. The hawk's breath grazed my back as I flew over the moat, ducked under the edge of the roof, and hurled myself into a tight corner, where I crouched, trembling and desperately wondering what defense I could use if my attacker crawled in after me.

The hawk didn't come. Yet I feared it might still be out there, perched on the roof, waiting with uncanny stillness for me to emerge. That didn't sound like normal hawk behavior, but I knew so little about them. By now I should've been an expert on any animal that wished to make me its supper. I'd grown careless, caught up in the novelty and excitement of flying. My first time out, I only hopped across the yard and took a short flight up into the nearest tree, growing accustomed to the odd sensation of seeing things behind me. With each day I flew, I grew bolder. I'd half-believed, half-hoped the magic lent me a kind of protective shield, keeping other animals from perceiving me. I knew better now. In future, I would watch for shadows, and feel for subtle shifts in the air that flowed around me.

Movement below caught my eye. Down on the castle lawn, six armed boarmen huddled together, speaking amongst themselves in snorts and grunts. Their pig heads with sharpened tusks were disturbing enough at the best of times, combined with the bodies of herculean men, broadened by thick padding covered in chain mail. Here, alone and unprotected at the castle, I shivered in dread, and shrank further into my corner. Their leader glanced upwards, revealing heavy scars across his eyes and snout. Even from this distance, or maybe because I knew the way they always looked at you, I felt the chill of his cold, black piggish eyes, devoid of feeling. Of course he wasn't looking at me, a little bird under the roof, but at an open window below me. Seconds later, a man extended his arm out the window and lowered it in signal.

The scarred boarman bellowed at another whose ear had been partly chewed off. The group opened up, revealing a frail man on his knees at their center, his hands tied behind his back. Pale and filthy with his clothing torn into strips, he looked as if they'd dragged him from the dungeon only moments earlier. Two of the boarmen lifted him to his feet and shoved him in the direction of the forest. His poor legs appeared weak and spindly from long disuse, but still he loped toward the trees, driven by a final, desperate hope that defied all logic. *If only I could help him.* But even if I flew down to lend him my wings, by the time I changed back, and before I could show the man what to do, the boarmen would surely have murdered us both.

Run, I silently urged. *Run as if the world were on fire beneath your feet.*

The boarmen salivated and raised their spears on their leader's command. The man stumbled just before reaching the trees, clawing his way up, fighting his way forward. *Faster! Don't give up!* The leader signaled for the boarmen to unleash their blood lust, and they pummeled each other to be first to their prey. They thundered across the field, hunched over and pig-like despite having the bodies of men. Their high-pitched squeals formed a grating war cry as they crashed through the bramble into the woods. Seconds later came a heartrending shriek that froze my blood. The trees shook during the killing frenzy that must have followed.

I couldn't bear to watch any longer. I set out from my refuge, meaning to fly directly home, but instead, curiosity drew me to the window below. I had to see with my own eyes the devil who had ordered that brutal execution. Landing on the sill in the corner, I told myself there was no danger because I looked like nothing but a harmless little bird. At worst he might swish me away, and I would fly off before his hand could touch me.

The man was Lord Fellstone himself. Stripped to the waist, he sprawled in a chair by the window, his feet propped on a low table, and his hands overloaded with jeweled rings. He looked as he had when I last saw him at the Midsummer celebration, with a mane of auburn hair that, considering his age, ought to be showing some grey. His nose was sharp, his eyes shrewd, his manner bored.

But it was the tall young woman beside him who drew my eye with her extraordinary appearance. She was dressed like a man, in close-fitting apparel sewn of dark green leather. She wore a cloth cowl of the same color round her head and neck, hiding her hair. A thin leather mask covered her forehead, cheeks, and the top of her nose, leaving open her mouth and chin. This woman hunched over Lord Fellstone, holding a sturdy, intricately carved wand of black wood. Its tip caught a beam of sunlight from the window and diffused it into a wide circle over a pustulent boil on Lord Fellstone's shoulder. The infection gradually cleared until it was gone. She moved the wand over a second boil that sprawled in a circle of virulent red near his waist.

His lordship raised his head and gave me such a piercing look, it caused the contents of my stomach to flip. His eyes widened in astonishment, until a loud, "Ha!" burst from him.

The woman paused. "My lord?" She followed his gaze to sparrow-me. I tried to leap into the air and fly away, but somehow I couldn't get my claws to let go of the sill. I didn't know if I was frozen in panic or rooted in place by a silent spell Lord Fellstone cast on me.

"Oh, I do love sparrows," he said. He leaned forward, his face growing animated. "You know, this one would make a splendid appetizer for my supper tonight."

"Boiled or roasted?" said the woman.

"Cooked over an open flame on a skewer, I should say. Fetch me my sword."

I couldn't believe my ears. No sensible person would ever eat a sparrow. For two tiny bites of stringy meat, it would not be worth all the trouble of plucking. *Is his lordship mad?* I strained to pull my feet away, while they stubbornly clung to the sill.

The woman lay down the wand and retrieved a sword with jewels encrusted on its handle.

"There won't be anything left of it after we spear it with that," Lord Fellstone said, making me wonder if he'd been playing with me all along. "Why is this bird still here anyway?" His lips curled into a smile that was ripe with evil intent.

My claws released and I shot up into the sky. I raced across the Cursed Wood and over the castle wall with one goal driving me: *get home.* Once during the flight, a shadow moved over me, but it was only a crow. As I reached the house and swooped down toward my window, the crow circled above and turned back the way we'd come. *Did the bird follow me?* I dismissed the thought as quickly as it occurred. My nerves were frayed; soon I'd be imagining eyes peering out of every tree.

The instant I touched my bedroom floor, I scraped three times with my claw. The familiar tingling sensation shot through me as I changed back into myself, Tessa Skye, sixteen years old, wearing a plain wool gown that laced up the front over my white shift. My key pouch hung from a belt that cinched my waist. It was odd how anything I wore or held onto when I changed into a bird would still be with me when I changed back, but magic was a powerful force beyond my understanding, and sometimes one had to simply accept what was, without being able to explain it.

I remained frozen for a moment, struck by the memory of that terrible hunt on the castle grounds. The shrill cry of the wretched man echoed still inside my head.

"Tessa."

I jumped and spun around at the sound of Papa's voice. He stood just behind me, framed by the doorway.

"Papa?" I said, giving him a blank look, masking my fear of what he might have seen.

His form seemed more gaunt than usual, his features stern and angular, his cheeks darkened with the stubble of three days' growth. His eyes fixed on the sparrow amulet that hung from my neck. Normally I tucked it out of sight under my gown, but I hadn't had time.

"Where did you get that?" he said.

I felt my face flush red, but I rallied, affecting a light tone. "I thought you'd gone out."

"The windrider," he said. "Tell me where it came from."

"The what?"

"Your amulet."

I hesitated before answering. "I found it."

"Where?"

"I don't recall."

"Don't tell me a falsehood. I know it was your mother's."

I wanted to bolt but he filled the doorway and I would never make it past him. "I remember now. She gave it to me," I said.

"No, she didn't," he said.

"How do you know?" A tinge of defiance crept into my voice.

"You were only four when she went away."

The old feelings of hurt and abandon rose. "I suppose she didn't love me enough to give me anything."

Papa scowled. "Don't talk nonsense. Tell me the truth. How did you get it?"

"I found it on her bedroom floor, the day she left," I said at last. "Was it so awful to take something that reminded me of her?"

"It's not a memento, it's a rare item of powerful magic. Give it to me."

I shrank back from him and clutched my throat. "No, Papa!" He had no idea what he was asking.

"You heard me. Magic is dangerous. Only the conjurers are allowed to use it. If it were up to me, it would be banished altogether."

"But you don't know... you've never felt... there's nothing else like it. Flying is pure and it makes me feel free, and.... How could anything be wrong with it?"

"You can be sure there's a price to be paid in using that magic. Not knowing what that price is makes it all the more troubling." He reached out his hand. "You're young yet. Be patient and good things will come, but not this way."

My eyes filled with tears as I lifted the necklace over my head and handed it to Papa. "I meant no harm."

He softened at the sight of my tears and clasped me to him. "Of course not. You didn't know the danger. Now you do. We'll speak no more of it." He held me for a moment. "Have you been to the Kettlemore's yet? We can't afford to scorn paid work."

I forced my gaze from the hand that clutched my sparrow. "Yes, Papa."

He had called it a windrider. The name suited my amulet; I would use it from now on. I would not despair of flying again, as I had my ways of bending Papa to my will over time. He simply didn't understand and I must find a way to convince him of the benefits. Perhaps he could be made to grasp its value by trying it himself. He would not want to, of course. And the truth was... I didn't want to let him use it. *It's mine and I should not have to share it.*

To learn more, please visit margiebenedict.com.

ALSO BY BY MARGIE BENEDICT

DREADMARROW (The Thieves of Magic Book One)

GRAVENWOOD (The Thieves of Magic Book Two)

KINGSHACKLE (The Thieves of Magic Book Three)

THE THIEVES OF MAGIC TRILOGY

BEFORE THE KILLING (The Killing Hour Book One)

BEFORE SHE WAS TAKEN (The Killing Hour Book Two)

BEFORE HE VANISHED (The Killing Hour Book Three)

THE KILLING HOUR BOOKS 1-3

INVADER

BLOOD AND VEIL

LAST GIRL STANDING

THE TRIALS

DEAD IN THE ROOM

NOT MY JOB ANYMORE

ACKNOWLEDGMENTS

Grateful thanks to these readers whose feedback helped me craft a stronger narrative: Leslie Andresen, Linda Dann Benevides, Peter L. Berg, Kris Broe, Alden Cox, Joyce F. Friedman, Sheila Kaplan, Kathy Miller, Carol Mitchell, Christine Murphy, Kathy Nezuh, Ellen Orne, Lauretta Prestera, Lisa Ryan, Ed Seksay, Elaine S. Suehnholz, and Margaret Wallace.

A big thank you to Alisa Kennedy Jones, publisher at Empress Editions, for her encouragement and insightful advice, and to Rodney Hatfield for expert guidance on branding.

Many thanks to the participants of the title selection contest: Ellen D'Antuono Blacklidge, Rolf Gjesteby, Sandra Hupp, Sheila Kaplan, Lisa Mammel, Terry Prescott Marshall, Lisa Dawn McMillan, Debbie Power, John Sadler, and Peter Silowan. You helped me find the perfect one.

To Ellen D'Antuono Blacklidge, CV Herst, Terry Prescott Marshall, Lauretta Prestera, John Sadler, and June Wolfe—thank you for stepping up as ARC (Advanced Reader Copy) readers. Your support is much appreciated.

A strong network of family and friends plays a huge part in keeping me motivated. Lia, Derek, Alan & Bridge, Sandra & Vernon, Lisa & Dean, Denise & Gordon, MaryEllen & Peter, Debbie & Bill, Karen & Stephen, Ansley & Peter, Lindsey &

George, Ed & Trish, Jane Carr, Sally, Julie, Rai, Catherine, Mimi, Nina, Cindy, Jane, Charlene, Cynthia, Linda, Eric, and Bianca—love you guys.

I'm grateful to Tony Overbay for his insightful podcast, *Waking up to Narcissism*, which woke me up—particularly the *Death by a Thousand Cuts* episodes. And to Riley Hope for her deeply resonating song, *Not My Job*, that Tony plays on his podcast.

Much love and gratitude for careful reading and positive critiquing goes to Tanner Kaptanoglu, Kay Liscomb, and Sheri Davenport. I'm so lucky to have you in my life.

Emma Hupp, thanks for your hard work, marketing savvy, and inspired ideas that helped my business grow. Sending love and wishing you mountains of success in your own author journey.

Jill L. Ferguson, I've always admired your talent and entrepreneurial spirit. Thank you for your help and support throughout our many years of friendship. I'm looking forward to joining you on your podcast.

Karla Sheridan, your meticulous reading of multiple drafts yielded corrections and advice as good or better than any professional editor might provide. But our long-lasting friendship is even more important to me. I literally can't ever thank you enough, dear friend.

Brian Charles Hupp, every morning I thank my lucky constellations that we found each other. You're my partner in every possibly way. You help me be the best version of myself with love, praise, and advice I admittedly don't always want to hear. You and Winston (*woof*) rock my world, baby.

ABOUT MARGIE BENEDICT

Margie Benedict writes emotionally resonant, genre-defying fiction rooted in the power of second chances. From coastal suspense to time-twisted mysteries and sweeping speculative worlds, her stories follow characters who rediscover their strength, reclaim their agency, and rewrite their destinies.

Formerly publishing as Marjory Kaptanoglu, Margie is the award-winning author of thirteen books praised by Kirkus, Publishers Weekly, and the BookLife Prize. Before turning to fiction full-time, she developed pioneering software at Apple Computer and wrote screenplays recognized by the Nicholl Fellowships and produced for film.

Margie is now building a brand readers can trust for gripping, transformative storytelling—books that don't just entertain but empower. From young adult fantasy to adult thrillers, sci-fi, and upmarket fiction, she invites readers of all ages to ask: *What would you do with a second chance?*